Just Another Tuesday in Manhattan

a journey of discovery

Authors note

In deciding how to write the story of Andy and Gino, I realised there would be an interesting language issue to tackle. The bulk of the story is based in New York, though as the British designer, Andy is the lead character, I took the decision that the narrative is largely with English spelling.

There are instances where US spelling has been used, largely for the native New Yorker characters. Andy makes reference to the sidewalk, riding the subway and other local vernacular as would happen naturally for someone working there for two years. I would expect that I use many of them, even as a visitor.

I hope that it adds an extra layer of interest for American readers, particularly in conveying Andy's place of being a Brit in a foreign land, with the narration reflecting that.

There are also some quite tough subjects dealt with in the story, of which I have no first-hand knowledge, but have researched. I apologise in advance for any inadvertent or even intentional factual inaccuracies which may have crept in to make the story flow; I have added some useful further reading at the end for readers to refer to. I didn't want to use this caveat as a 'spoiler' so hopefully this will make sense as you read through the story

I hope you will enjoy the story and feel as bought into the characters as I have while writing it. Please do feel free to send me your feedback. I'm always grateful for others' views.

Just Another Tuesday in Manhattan

Christopher Tradgett

"He is admirably upbeat in his writing, which is cheerful, affectionate, articulate and instantly accessible - and no small portion of warmth and optimism... Christopher Tradgett has impressed me with this one, and left me keen to read more from him. Take a look; you'll enjoy it, I'm sure." **Matt McAvoy**, Goodreads reviewer

Contents

$$— 1 —$$

Another Tuesday Morning

Andy took the same M train subway, at the same time each morning, from the 65th St station in the Woodside area of Queens heading into Manhattan. It was just a twenty-minute ride in, to arrive at the specialist design studio on East 37th Street, just off the famous Madison Avenue - in the heart of the agency district.

This Tuesday was no different - just another Tuesday. Riding the subway gave him the chance to listen in to podcasts, like the 'Resourceful Designer' and the 'Logo Geek'; there was always something to make him think about how he approaches some design issue or other in packaging or branding.

Glancing up at the faces of the others in the car, they were all immersed in their own audio worlds, into their tunes, heads nodding or in a podcast world, like himself.

His route into town emerged into daylight by Bryant Park, into another of those bright Manhattan mornings. He'd grown to love the short walk through the wide green open space, stopping at his favoured coffee stand for a Macchiato. Somehow the trees around the pathways seemed to have a calming effect - the regular faces around him that he'd come to recognise, looking way more chilled than those on the street, sipping their coffees and soaking up the last of the early morning glow.

Other commuters were pausing to sit and read newspaper headlines, to meet friends, or just take a breath before starting their day. Others were on a cooling-down jog across the grass or doing their final stretches after the morning run.

It felt kind of… almost insulated from the noise of the traffic - and the sidewalks, packed with intense sharp suited types, all seemingly on a mission, heading to the offices which towered around them.

This was of course, a very different vibe to living in south London and the design agency off Balham High Street, or even to London's West End where he'd almost taken a job at one of the famous global agencies. But he'd chosen this one, here at 'The Packsmiths' agency in central Manhattan, and he'd really warmed to the whole New York lifestyle over his nearly two years here.

He set off the few blocks south, to dive back into the hustle of the street, towards his agency building and his design studio.

Andy crossed over the street and heard a shout behind him, "Hey," which made him look back over at the tall guy with a moustache, in a green Yankees cap, who was looking straight at him, waving to him, calling out - "Hey, Hey Gino! See you later in Dillon's - I'm going to try and bring Michelle along too."

Andy did a bit of a double take - not sure if he recognised him from somewhere - and was wondering why the guy was calling at him! He tried to call back, but the traffic had moved on, with delivery vans now blocking his view. He thought again, the guy had absolutely been talking to him, but, Gino? What's that about…?

His curiosity was definitely piqued, and being how he was, he couldn't just dismiss it, so he fought his way back across the street, through the jam. He had to find out who this guy was and how he thought he knew him. But looking in all directions for a hat and 'tache, he drew a blank. The guy had just disappeared among the faces coming along the sidewalks and through the park.

So, did the guy know him, or had he mistaken him for someone called Gino (or Geno with an e maybe)? Still searching in vain for the green cap, Andy took a sip of his coffee, before giving up and going back across the street on his way to work.

It had taken just a few seconds - but had him thinking. So, should he recognise the guy with the 'tache? Maybe they'd met in a club or one of the bars - but he couldn't pin it down to anything recently. Plus, 'Andy' could never have been misheard as 'Gino/Geno'! Perhaps he just looked a bit like the guy's friend Gino, perhaps? A trick of the light maybe. Who knows?

Andy pushed the door into the agency building on E 37th, swiped in and took the elevator to the 9th floor. He shared a cheery 'good morning' with Serena at reception and headed across the studio to his desk. While he waited for the Mac to power up, he went over the strange encounter he'd just had with his friend Denny, working on the desk next to him.

Denny couldn't place a guy with a green cap and moustache, based on Andy's description, certainly not in the agency world around here. He had hit it off pretty well with Denny on the workstation next to him straight away after coming to The Packsmiths. They were similar ages and backgrounds and had similar routes into the product and pack design specialism, though Denny had moved here from a small town outside Raleigh, in North Carolina.

If the guy earlier was someone Andy had randomly met before, then it may be worth following up - it doesn't harm having options to grow your network in this town. It was a puzzler.

Andy opened up the day's work list in the Jira scheduling app - and looked blankly at it, as he asked himself, "So, who was that guy - and Gino? That must have been the name he had called out." He took a quick look through LinkedIn at New York contacts with a 'tache in their profile pic but couldn't see anything resembling the guy earlier.

It was rather intriguing. He could of course just ignore it and move on - that wasn't going to happen, so how should he follow it up and see where it leads?

"OK, Denny," Andy resolved, thinking out loud, "I know I'm a bit obsessive, and I'd just stew over it, so I just have to find out what's going on," addressing Denny, "so, OK, he must have been talking about the Peter Dillon's Irish bar on 36th, the next street down. That has to be it. However, I ask you…" turning to face him and raising his finger, "when, exactly, is 'later' going to be?"

Denny laughed, "Sounds like you've really had a weird one there, man. Obsessive or not, I'd say it makes sense to find out who the guy was - could be a 'career useful' type contact - and you must have met him somewhere, I guess."

The decision only took a moment, "OK, I'm decided," he resolved, "I just can't *not* go there 'later'- whenever that is; maybe I'll find out who that was and how this guy thinks he knows me. I'm thinking I'll do an early shoot this afternoon and go hang out in Dillon's, just to see if he turns up - and take it from there."

It was probably going to be worth that small effort - at very least, he'll maybe be useful to know, "…and if you're curious, you can join me when you're done here. Worst case scenario - at least we can have a few beers together, if it turns out to be a wild goose chase."

Tuesday felt like a very long day - mainly because the jobs on today's list didn't really get the creative juices flowing. Three jobs adapting existing packaging, labelling and box artwork to a slightly smaller size of a series of product flavors - the joys of shrinkflation. And editing the existing product merchandising brochure, with new shelf barkers - in the vain hope to make the smaller products appear not to be any smaller!

What had happened to his lofty ambitions, branching out from the small South London agency for a life of cutting-edge creativity here in the heart of New York's Adland? Much of the actual work was similar - but just on much bigger brand names.

Plus, there's the new work that punctuates the run of the mill stuff. The occasional full brand refresh, exhibition graphics and exhibition stand design, which can have an almost architectural component. But it's the opportunity to work on projects that touch thousands or even millions of lives that still fired Andy. Even these simple packaging changes - they'll be appearing in thousands of grocery stores across the US and Canada.

Checking the time later on, he saw it was 4:30 already and he'd worked through most of the jobs in less time than he'd expected.

Amending the work cards with the timings to 'DONE' in Jira for billing, Andy closed down his Mac for the day. Collecting his stuff together, he made for the door, "This is it, I'm off," way ahead of his usual time, to station himself in Dillon's Bar to find out whenever 'later' was.

Denny looked up as Andy waved, "I'll join you later man, when I've finished this last job. Is there a Newcastle soccer match on the TV there again?"

Andy said he'd take a look, they were always entertaining to watch even for a neutral supporter, and Dillon's was the official home of the Newcastle United 'Toon Army' in Manhattan. Much the same as the Football Factory was the home of Chelsea, his dad's team - which he also followed, but not seriously. It looked like a good spot to meet up with other ex-pats from London though, and he'd made a couple of good friends there.

But - this was about seeing the guy with the 'tache, and see why he thought he recognised him - maybe find out more about him, if he might be useful to know - and whoever Gino was, if there was one - and if it doesn't happen, then it's a couple of beers with Denny, which will be good anyway before heading to the gym.

2

Tuesday - 'later'

Taking a first sip of his Guinness, Andy made for a seat at the beer barrel table in the centre of the bar area - the ideal way to end the work day as well. It was good to know that this was a proper drop of the black stuff, still brewed in the Dublin brewery. Despite the Newcastle connection here, he'd never really got on with the Geordies' legendary Brown Ale. So it was Guinness - after all, this was an Irish Pub!

The barrel table was also the perfect vantage point to spot anyone coming in the door. He guessed there couldn't be a live game this evening like the FA Cup game he caught with Denny a while back. A poster listed the upcoming fixtures, mostly early morning, which made sense for a 3pm UK kick off. There was a rerun showing on the big screens however, of the home game against Liverpool from earlier in the season.

Dillon's was pretty quiet but it was early still - just before 5, so hopefully he'd be in good time for whenever 'later' was going to be. That could be any time after work, he guessed, so he'd better pace himself. He overheard a few British accents around him, mostly blokes, but no Geordie voices that he could hear. He settled down with his Guinness, put his earbuds in and went back to listening to the podcast from this morning, glancing at the door and then up at the football now and then - and waited.

A few people came and went while he was sat there, none he recognised which wasn't that unusual he supposed. After just over half an hour, Andy glanced up and spotted the tall guy with the 'tache coming in off the street, sharing a joke with his friend -

who looked to be about his own height, with dark red-brown hair, similar to his own - and at first glance, could be Andy's double.

As they came closer, it was clear that the only difference between them, that Andy could see, was that his hair was styled and shorter, and that he looked to be a sharp dresser, in a quality suit.

The tall guy scanned the bar and visibly stopped in his tracks and did a double take as he spotted Andy staring at them - looked back to his friend, who followed his gaze as he looked back - and, almost comically, both just froze, mouth open and wide-eyed.

Andy stood up - in the same, almost cartoon pose.

Now it was obvious why he'd been mistaken for the friend - who must be the Gino he thought he'd been calling out to this morning.

After what seemed like an age, they came over towards him; Andy and Gino stared at each other.

"What the…?"

"Er… I was thinking the exact same thing!" Andy took in his features, same green eyes, same colour hair, same dimpled chin. He reached out to shake hands, "I'm Andy Jordan - and I'm guessing you must be Gino?"

"Yeah - Gino Bianchi - what the?... How do you know me? - and hell, how - why do we look… so alike? Though, it sounds like you're British, am I right? This is so - just weird," looking back at his friend, "I was thinking, is this your idea of a joke, Max? But… hell, I was a bit confused when you said you'd seen me this morning…" staring again at Andy, "and now it's plain to see why… jeez!"

"Hell yeah!"

"And that's how you knew I was Gino…"

Andy nodded, "yep. And that's what brought me here this afternoon - it's Max, is it? You were looking straight at me and shouted over the street, 'see you later in Dillons'. I just had to follow that up and find out more."

"Yeah, too right I did… Whew! That must have spooked you - now we're all about as confused as each other!"

Andy was still taking in Gino's face, "...and you're from round here, from the sound of it. How… were you born here? - it's like we're kind of doppelgangers? I'm thinking it's surprising we've not been mistaken for each other before... Though, then again, I've only been living here a couple of years, so maybe it's not."

"Hey, this is a big buzzing city - and no Gino, this ain't no joke." Max looked from one to the other. "I can't believe what I'm seeing here. Now, I've gotta work this out - but first, I think I need a drink - you too Gino, Andy, Guinness, is it?" asked Max, as he headed for the bar for some beers, "I think we'll *all* need one."

To break the ice, Andy told Gino how he'd moved to New York to work, as a packaging designer at an agency on the next street - and that he was around this area all the time, or where he lived, in Queens, in a rental apartment near Woodside.

Gino gave Andy a brief outline as well; that he was in real estate, remodeling and leasing up town near Columbus Circle, mostly swanky overpriced apartments near the park. "I often meet up with Max and the guys here, so yeah, it's really strange this hasn't happened 'til now. And, hey, I live in Astoria in Queens, so we can only live about a mile or two apart! So, yeah, it's amazing we've not come across each other before."

Max came back with the beers, "OK, OK, so guys - I need to get my head round this... Andy, so you're definitely a Brit, I take it," Andy nodded, "and Gino, I know you're from Queens - hell, we grew up together..." he paused to think, "There's like, seven billion people on this planet and you're right Andy, I've heard stories where people have a doppelganger who looks a bit similar, like you said. But from where I'm standing - as the one who can see you both, you're not just similar. You two are so alike - you could even be twins!"

Gino looked at Andy "That's a crazy idea Max. How would that work?"

Max pointed at each of them, "Similar age, same height, same hair colour, same chin. So, let's take a test. OK Andy: you're a dead ringer for Gino - and you both look a similar age, so as a start, what's your date of birth?"

"Well, you already know my birthday is 3 August, you send me a card every year. Born in 1981."

Andy just stared at him "Er... and same here - 3rd of August - nineteen... eighty... one."

Max almost shouted "Holy crap!!" - startling the group stood next to them watching the football, "Sheesh! I did not expect that! Now, that's *never* just a random coincidence, it just can't be! No way! So much for my test. So how does that happen?"

Andy's mind was racing while Max was speaking, "Just an idea Gino, but were you by any chance adopted?"

"I was, yes… I've known my whole life. I grew up in Queens, but don't know much about where I actually came from. Adoption was never something we discussed - or that I even thought about - we're too close a family for it to have been a thing really."

"Same here. I was adopted too, but my Mum told me some of the details years ago, about me being born in Dublin but I don't remember everything as it didn't seem important. So I'm not totally sure either."

"Oh man! That's got me thinking, Andy - same birthday and both adopted… I am just gonna have to call my mom and find out what else she knows and see if it ties in - this minute. Oh wow!"

He couldn't have been more agitated, "hey, I've an idea - Andy, can I get a photo of the both of us to send to mom? - I just have to talk to her," angling for a good double selfie, "Now this photo might just totally freak her out - but guaranteed it will make her call back. How should I put it," he typed, "so, 'guess who I bumped into?' - that should do it. And, here goes!" as he hit send.

About 20 seconds later, Gino's phone rang. He smiled, "Yep, mom took the bait," and headed for the door to take the call.

Andy suggested another round of beers, "I've a feeling we might need it!" He headed to the bar, with his mind turning over what was happening here. 'It's just not something that happens - you don't just discover a twin - a brother like that'. He rejoined Max with refills in hand.

"I guess Andy, you wondered who the heck I was this morning?"

"Too right! it was just so clear that you were looking directly at me - I tried to cross over and find out what you were saying. I was thinking maybe we'd met at some agency event or something, but you'd just disappeared."

"Yeah, I was in such a rush heading to a meeting. If I'd thought about it, I shoulda known somethin' was up if it had been Gino hangin' around Bryant - it's well outside his usual pitch. But now I see you both together, it's no surprise I mistook you."

While Gino was outside on the phone, Denny arrived and came over to them from the bar, "holy shit Andy, that was so weird, bud. I just saw a guy looking a bit like you outside, talking on the phone - no wonder he just ignored me!" he laughed.

Following right behind him, Gino was just finishing his call and came back to join them, "Oh wow, guys! You gotta listen to this."

Denny turned - and just stared at them both. "Gino, this is Denny, my mate from work. Denny - Gino. And Max, as you can see here, is the guy who called out to me this morning."

"Oh shit man! - Who's… You didn't tell me about a… a brother, is it?" Denny was looking from face to face, "I was thinking this was just going to be a mistaken identity thing, bud!"

Gino laughed, "Hey, good to meet you Denny. Oh boy! Have you just stumbled into the twilight zone here!" as he turned back to Andy and Max, "Now, listen up… Well - man, that was *very* interesting. I've learned more from Mom about my adoption in the last three minutes than literally any time before in my life," as Denny continued to look open mouthed, from one face to the other.

"…and?" Max prompted, impatiently, "OK, come on - what have you found out?"

"Andy, how much do you know about your adoption?" Gino asked, smiling.

"As I said, I was probably born in Dublin. I grew up in south London - in Brixton, but I know I was adopted via an Irish Catholic charity that Grandma had suggested - she was a strong Catholic - and I might have been born in or around Dublin. I don't know a great deal more - though Mum always said that's where I got my hair colour. She will know all the details I'm sure."

"Okay - well Andy, I think you'd better put your beer down… Mom really opened up to me just now - and I'm sure I've not heard any of this before. They too had adopted me from a Catholic charity, would you believe - based in Dublin!"

Max stared at them both, "Is there likely to be more than one over there? - I guess it's a pretty catholic country so there could be a load of them. But what if it was the same place..."

"When mom saw that photo of us two - I was right, it sure did blow her mind! She'd had no idea about other children there at the time, let alone one who could be a twin. I was the only child she'd seen there - and the nuns had not mentioned anything. You may well have been there at the same time. It just has to be that we're twins - there's no way that could have been two different charities surely."

Andy nodded, "That seems to make total logical sense Gino. Dublin's not that big a place either, though the only time I've been there was on a stag weekend, so we didn't see that much of the city, just the pubs around Temple Bar and the river."

Andy gestured with his phone, "Can you share that photo with me, Gino? I'd love to send it to my mum. I am just going to have to call her in the morning. It's a bit late over there now, and I might just prime her first before sending it over - don't want to spook her, like you did to your mom! I can hopefully find out what other information she's got, like the name of the charity. What else did your mother have?"

"Well, I now know my Mom and Pop flew over to finalize the adoption legalities at the charity in Dublin and then flew home with me, when I was just a few weeks old" Gino caught brief flashes from his childhood running through his head as he thought through what was happening here.

Max laughed, "There's a delicious irony in discovering a Dublin adoption story, drinking Guinness in the middle of an Irish bar! Michelle will be so pissed at missing all this - she missed it all for another evening of jazz."

"...and Andy says we yanks don't understand irony! Hey," Denny put his arm around both of them, "you guys are going to have to get a DNA test. The likeness is just, well... and your birthdates it's just - so obvious," as he looked between the two identical faces, "but you'll want to know 100%, I'm sure."

"Good call Denny," Max suggested, "you guys should swap deets, if you are related somehow - then you two are gonna need to stay in touch."

Andy and Gino exchanged numbers, "thanks Gino. I'm going to have to shoot soon. I've actually got a yoga session booked at the gym later on - but I'm thinking that we'll be speaking to each other quite a bit from now on. I'll phone my mum in the morning - then call you around breakfast time, just before 8, if that works for you."

"Sounds perfect Andy. Holy cow, I'm still trying to get my head around all this. Mind. Blown! Eh Max?"

"100% - this is the weirdest random pub conversation I've ever been sucked into. I can't wait to find out more."

Andy and Denny got up to leave the two friends, "I'll give you a call in the morning after I've talked with my mum. Speak to you soon - my maybe brother!"

"Can't wait Andy - speak to you then."

They left Gino and Max, still looking shellshocked, back to the subway past Bryant Park, which was now almost in darkness, Andy thought through what had just happened - feeling the same way that Gino looked as he'd left. This was the most unsettling thing he'd encountered for some while.

If Gino was in fact a lost twin and they were separated at birth, that opens a whole new experience to deal with - and a new type of dynamic between them. Twins' psychology was not something he'd ever thought he'd need to know about.

One thing was certain, he knew for sure that he'll be speaking to Gino again. That was after talking to Mum - now that was going to be an interesting conversation.

3

Tuesday evening

Gino called his mom again later that evening, to talk through the rest of what he knew about Andy Jordan. She read through a few of the details she'd dug out, just after Gino had called from his strange encounter in the Irish bar, and they talked more about his adoption, traveling to Dublin to collect him as a baby - and more of his childhood.

He shared what he had found out so far about what Andy knew of his adoption; it seemed impossible that it was only a few hours ago that they first met.

The idea of the two of them possibly being twins had come as a big shock to his mom. She had stared at that photo of the two boys ever since he'd sent it. Gino was picking up that she was feeling a bit unsettled. A sense of remorse, maybe for being a part of the two of them having been separated, if indeed that was what happened, though she didn't voice it directly.

He told her that he and Andy were thinking of going to a DNA testing clinic. "What do you think about it - would you be OK with that?"

"Don't be so silly Gino, you just have to. The two of you have the same birth date and as I can see from that photo, looking so alike is plain as - well, the noses on your faces - and the dimples on your chins!" she laughed. "I was going to suggest it anyways, there is so much to… to get your heads around. Has Andy spoken to his mother yet?"

"He's calling her in the morning - it was too late over in England. He said he'd send her that photo - *after* he tells her about me and all that happened today. He didn't want to give her the same shock as I gave you!" he smiled. "Sorry again about that, it was just - just such a bombshell. I literally had to share it with you."

"I get that, dear, you were always a bit impulsive," she smiled to herself.

Gino told her how, when they were talking earlier, he had flashes of his childhood running through his mind. Moving house to house, while Dad tried to grow the building business - moving into the first finished apartment in each building as they renovated it. "Fun times, eh?"

"Not without some tricky moments as well, son," she came back, "we were often almost over our heads in debt in those early days."

"But you always… it never seemed that way, you always made life exciting Mom. It always felt solid to me."

"If only you knew… though I guess you understand a lot more now you've been running real estate businesses yourself. Ah well, I guess it has been fun in the long run."

"I'm going to have to come and see you out on the Island, perhaps at the weekend and take a look at what other documents you've got there."

"That'll be great - we can do some searching together, son."

Gino said his goodbyes and Max called straight after, "Hey bud, your phone's been busy."

"Yeah, I just got off speaking to mom again and telling her more about Andy and everything. Interestingly, she's really cool on the DNA test, in fact she said she was going to suggest it herself."

"Sweet. That makes things easier - you've gotta hope Andy's mother feels the same when he tells her." Max added, "hey, shame that Michelle didn't show up as well, that really would have complicated things even more."

"Yeah, yeah, Max. I know you're still trying to pair us two off. I'm still not sure we really click whenever we've dated, to be honest."

After his call with Max, Gino did a search online for DNA clinics to see what options there were - and which were quickest. There seemed to be so many different types - more than he expected, and only a few quoted prices for their tests. Ones without prices claimed a quick service was guaranteed, which no doubt meant that they would cost more. But hey, he - they - needed to find out for certain.

He messaged Andy, letting him know his mom's support for them doing the test and he'd do some more research on the DNA clinics, and would call him in the morning if that works for him. Andy replied straight away - 'that's great, I'll have spoken with my mum by then as well. Let's get this set up asap!'

Mom's thoughts

"That boy! He truly is my life now that I've lost Joe. It's been a tough couple of years I guess but I'm blessed to have my Gino - along with all my friends in the Church and my walking group pals.

"Joe was such a strong guy - building that business up from next to nothing all those years ago. Talking with Gino just then brought that all back. It's just so, so sad that the construction work he loved was what killed him - all that damned asbestos they used to use. Who knew…?

"I do know that he was so proud that Gino picked up the construction bug and ran with it - even if it was more the interiors side of things. He's made such a success of it. We always wondered where he'd gotten his creative flair from; it wasn't me - and certainly not Joe!

"Yes, I can count myself as truly blessed."

— 4 —

Wednesday phoning Mum

After a strange and fitful night's sleep, Andy woke very early, unsurprisingly, and went for an early morning walk around the streets of Woodside to clear his mind, before breakfast and calling his mum. His wandering through the pre-dawn stillness took him past quiet homes, some with lights on where people were stirring for an early start to the day.

He passed the Filipino cafes and grocery stores which gave rise to the local name of Little Manila, all still in darkness. He was trying to process all that had happened and had been said, only a few hours ago and almost felt like it had been a weird dream… but it wasn't - he had met Gino, and it seemed to change everything. Turning back into his own street, he felt brighter and clearer in his mind - more prepared to have that call with his mother.

Cup of tea in hand, he face-timed his mother in England, it was just after 11 when Jeannette's phone rang.

"This is a bit early for you Andrew, it can only be about what, it's not even six in the morning there. What's up - are you all right?" He gently introduced the news about meeting Gino the previous evening. Well, as gently as it was possible in the circumstances, before sending her Gino's 'twin' photo, while they were talking. He covered meeting Gino in the bar and him looking similar and what had come out about his adoption, and then sent the photo across to her phone…

"Oh, my word! That… Andrew, that is just uncanny," she said, "given what you just told me about his adoption - and that photo, you two really can't be anything but twins. Even looks like you have the same hair colour. And for once I'm glad you wear it longer, or it would be hard to tell you apart, at least from this photo. From what you've found out so far, it sounds like the facts here seem so clear and yes, you'll have to do that DNA test and really make sure of it, love."

"I was hoping you'd be OK with us doing that."

"Absolutely Andrew, don't be daft!" she looked thoughtful for a moment, "I'm just mortified. I feel terrible that by adopting you, we might have been responsible for splitting up a pair of twins, if that's what's happened here. That would never be allowed nowadays of course."

Andy shared what he knew so far of Gino's background, and the conversations they'd had so far, even though it was only 12 hours since he'd first seen him.

"That day when we adopted you and brought you home to our flat in Brixton it was the happiest day of my life. After we'd been married a few years, I thought we'd never be able to have children - and as you know, because you came from the agency in Dublin, that was why we kept the name the nuns gave you, Patrick, as your middle name."

"Your Dad had had misgivings. He'd wanted to adopt a child of mixed heritage. 'To make it feel more natural' he'd said - though I still think that came mostly from Granny Carmine. You're going to have to call him as well and tell him the news. He's still on the same mobile number - oh and you must let Leon know all about it too. It will be good for him to hear all this from the horse's mouth - and you two need to talk more often anyway. They're both going to be as amazed as I am."

Andy's Dad, Joseph Jordan, was born in Barbados in '52 and came to the UK in the early 60s with his parents George and Carmine to live in Brixton. One of the few areas of London they could settle in. Across many other parts of London, rented flats were frequently advertised as 'No Irish, no dogs, no blacks', so Brixton and that area of London felt welcoming. Joseph had a happy time growing up in Brixton.

Andy's Mum, Jeannette, trained as a nurse in Essex and had been working in King's College Hospital in Camberwell and sharing a house with other nurses just off Coldharbour Lane in Brixton, initially sharing the flat with her nurse friends. She met Joseph through friends on a Saturday night out at the Clouds club and married soon afterwards and had an exciting few years enjoying the club culture.

After moving in together, they soon were able to move to their own place, down nearer Brixton's centre, with its rich Caribbean culture - and just round the corner from the Crown and Anchor of course. It was to this home that Jeannette and Joseph brought their new baby Andrew.

The family moved house to Morden later on, when Dad transferred from the Victoria to the Northern Line, to a proper little house and then Leon came along to complete the family.

Though Andy's parents had separated a while back, Mum was still living in their house on Central Road, not far from the park he'd hung around in as a teenager.

"All this has set me off wondering what it would have been like growing up with a twin brother - if that's what we turn out to be."

"I know Andrew. I'm going to have to dig through all the papers in the adoption file - and that other box of stuff in the loft and see what I can find. I've got some reading to do. If this turns out as I think it might when you get the test results, it would be nice to come over and see you, earlier than we had planned, and meet this chap Gino as well, if you think that's the right thing to do."

"That would be great, I'm sure he'd be keen to meet you - and thanks Mum for just... being you. Sorry to have dropped a bombshell on you on a Wednesday morning - and you're right what you said earlier, this could be life changing."

After his call, and before phoning Leon or Dad, Andy reflected on the fact that he'd gone from knowing who he was and his place in the world, to where he now found himself, it had been less than a day - but he was now facing an entirely other view on his life, and wanting to understand more about what happened before being adopted. Not least, there was the thought that Gino and he could be actual twins - that was a whole other world view!

Gino had had a similar restless night, and he too woke early. Coffee in hand, he opened his laptop and started looking again at the options for DNA testing. Never having had an interest in any of this, it came as a bit of a surprise that there were so many clinics for paternity or family history testing. There were a few local ones around Queens, but he found that they'd probably get a quicker service and test results across in Manhattan. He narrowed it down to a clinic in Midtown, on E 71st, which seemed to promise the fastest service.

He had also called his mom before breakfast as well, and she had expressed how sad it was that his dad, Joe, had missed all of this. In the couple of years since he'd died, he'd left a huge hole in his life - and even more so for his mom.

After the conversation with his mum, Gino called Andy, "Good morning, Andy Jordan. I've just gotten off the phone with mom again, who is so excited about us going for a test. I guess you have too - how is your mom about it?"

"Yes, indeed Gino Bianchi! I had a long chat with her about family and stuff - and going for the DNA test, which she's 100% behind us on. She's going to go through all the adoption papers and see what else she can find. If the test results do what we're all expecting, she said she'd love to come here and meet you - if you're OK with the idea."

"Absolutely Andy, it'd be great to meet her. Mom said she was going to do the same digging, up in the attic. And hey, I just know she'd love to meet her too if she's coming over - Jeannette, wasn't it?"

Just before he left for the office, he phoned his brother Leon, to let him know what had happened, and his conversation with mum, "and she seems to be fine with us doing the DNA research. She's also thinking of coming over to meet Gino, if it goes how we're expecting. Would you want to come over with her?"

"I'm sure I can do it. And looking at that photo of the two of you - that is something I'm going to have to see in real life, or I'd swear it was photoshopped!" they both laughed, "And mum's not done much flying recently, so I'd love to come over with her. This all sounds just wild, for you and Gino."

"Great, I'll keep you in the loop as well then." He then called his dad to get him up to speed on what had happened to him the previous day.

Thinking through all the conversations he'd had just this morning on the subway ride into work, he realised he had no idea what the podcast he'd been playing was about. His mind was turning over everything about meeting Gino the previous evening, and his conversations this morning.

After swiping into the building and taking the elevator up to the Packsmiths studio, he sat down and filled Denny in on his calls with his mum and Gino just earlier. "Was it really only this time yesterday that it all started?"

"Like Gino said - you guys are in some kind of twilight zone til you work it all out."

Life was not going to be the same again. But for now, it was time to log on to Jira, and get some work done - and today at last, a more creative project to get his teeth into.

Mum's thoughts

"It changed our lives, it did. Adopting Andrew made us into the family we'd both always hoped for, ever since we first got together. I thought it would never happen, though the doctors hadn't found any problems that would stop me conceiving. The idea of adoption was a suggestion from Nan, as her priest had suggested this Dublin agency and then it all seemed to fall into place.

"Joseph doted on their 'Andy Pandy', as he called him, after the TV puppet he grew up watching. His shock of dark red hair as a baby always got attention, especially when he was out with Joseph. Luckily for us, Brixton was a real cultural melting pot, so we fitted in just fine. And then four years later, Leon came along - what a surprise! Granny Carmine had got her wish for a mixed-race child after all.

"It was of course a sad break when Joseph and I separated a few years back, after Michael had left home. But... we'd grown apart and had

nothing left in common, and we both had our own groups of friends. I'm glad that we're still good friends though.

"And I've got two gorgeous boys to fuss over. And maybe another now!"

— **5** —

Wednesday - making plans

It almost seemed strange to Gino to be heading off to the office. He was thinking through how he'd had a real change in his mindset since meeting Andy - less than a day ago. The idea of an actual brother - a brother he'd always wanted when growing up, as his mom had reminded him, was a whole new experience for him.

He called the clinic he'd found online soon after 9am and managed to book a slot for the DNA test for noon on Friday, and messaged Andy to let him know and asked if he was free for another quick call.

That in itself was unusual for him as he usually preferred messaging, though of course in the office, he was never off the phone. Apart from work it was mostly his mom or older relatives he phoned. But it seemed natural to want to share what he'd been thinking about his dad with Andy.

"Jeez, Andy. I can't believe it was only a day ago - no half a day ago that we met. It's still blowing my mind. I'm not sure I slept; my mind was just buzzing."

"I know Gino, I was up so early I went for a walk in the dark to clear my mind before calling Mum - she asked what's wrong - is everything OK!"

They laughed, "that's just what Mom would think with an early phone call. Hey, for that DNA test, how about we meet up midday Friday, just outside the clinic?"

"Makes sense Gino - and yeah, it seems just so weird that it was only yesterday. My head's been running on overdrive. That walk before phoning Mum this morning, was to work through what the hell had just happened - to get it clear in my head."

"I get that. When I spoke with Mom this morning, it sounded as though she's as excited about all this as I am - we both are, I guess?"

"And I'd certainly count my Mum in that frame of mind as well now!"

"Mom reminded me that it was nearly two years since my dad passed away. He'd have loved to know what is happening now."

"Wow, that's tough Gino, I don't know how to… what to say. That's… so sad to hear."

"Hey, thanks. But he'd had lung and breathing problems for years through working with asbestos in the construction business. Quite a few of his friends in construction had the same problems, especially the roofers, as so many older houses used asbestos shingles. The disease later on led to a carcinoma in his left lung. He only lasted a year after that diagnosis, so we'd had a few years of knowing he'd not last for ever." Andy didn't know how to respond but tried to think how he'd feel if it had been his own dad.

"Mom was saying that it was a shame he's not still around to hear our story - though she's convinced he'll be looking down on us. She's feeling pretty much alone these days, I guess. She's got a good friends network around her, volunteering at St Rocco's church thrift clothing store; and she has her walking group she meets up with every week with lots of other ladies 'of a certain age'. She keeps pretty busy."

Gino filled Andy in on his years growing up with Max as his best friend and living in Queens. They'd both been at the same high school, and both their fathers had been in the construction industry, so their families often met socially.

"How was your own adoption?"

"I've had a great life. I always knew I'd been 'chosen', as Mum put it. I was just a normal kid growing up. Four years later she had my brother Leon - she reckons all the pressure was off and nature took its course.

"Oh wow, that must have been great - I wish my mom had had that. I think I always knew she'd have liked a bigger family, and she said she'd have loved for me to have a brother to play with. I've a lot of cousins - Mom's sisters and Dad's sister all had bigger families but they weren't close by to us. I guess she felt a bit… left behind maybe?"

"I get that - must be hard - my mum had one sister, with my two cousins Kelly and Paul, so she'd not had that pressure, I suppose. My Dad's work was less glamorous than yours sounds. He's - rather, he was a tube train driver til he retired, first on the Victoria Line when we lived in Brixton, then we moved to Morden when he transferred to the Northern Line trains. I ended up going to Art College and then worked at a printers and a few design studios around London before moving over here. How about you?"

"I guess I followed in my father's footsteps, almost. I'm a partner in a real estate business, and we basically take on older apartments and remodel them. My partner manages the business side of things and I cover the design and interiors side - we make a good team. I guess it really is an extension of what my dad was doing."

"That sounds like major league, to me."

"Not really, as my pop helped to set us up in business years ago to buy our first apartment and showed us how to 'flip' to generate some capital. Now it's more about adding value - beautiful European style bathrooms and kitchens really sell a place in Manhattan and get higher rentals."

"So we're both pretty artsy then - both practical applied art really. You on interiors and me designing packaging and stuff for in-store promotions."

"I guess so. Well, we should get to find out for sure on Friday who we really are - or a bit after that. Max is suggesting we meet up when we've picked up the test results, to keep them in the loop. I think he's as excited as me to find out about all this. Anyhow, I'm going to have to get an early night - I've an early meeting up state in the morning."

"Anyhow, I suppose I'd better get back to doing some actual work here. Great talking to you fella. See you Friday - 'High Noon' eh?"

"Ha ha, yeah - see you there."

— 6 —

Friday DNA testing

Friday morning came round quicker than expected in this fast-moving week and it took all of his usual calming walk through Bryant Park with the end of the podcast episode, to chill enough to head to the studio. He swiped in and after getting settled at his desk, he turned to Denny, "Today's the day mate! I'm taking an early lunch to meet Gino uptown for our DNA tests at noon. Here's hoping that'll make things clearer."

"I'll bet this wasn't something you'd had in your plan moving to New York - or even a week ago! But - this really could be quite something for you, bud. Hey, I've been thinking it would make a great Instagram, or a YouTube channel - 'Separated twins reunited', maybe."

"I think we'd better find out if it's true first of all! But it's a cool idea." Later that morning, Andy waved to Serena as he left the office, before taking a walk towards Grand Central, for the subway uptown to meet Gino, on E 71st at the clinic.

Gino held the door for Andy as they went in to register for the test. At the desk, the receptionist kept looking at their Social Security and Passports - she glanced back up, "I'm not sure what to make of this - so you are totally separate." Andy gave a brief intro to his and Gino's story.

"Wow, that's a first for me. I've not come across separated twins before. Different passports and nationalities. But," she shrugged, "I guess the DNA data won't lie - so we should be able to establish the facts either way for you both, in a few days - though looking at the pair of you, I would hazard that there's pretty strong odds you're connected," as she ushered them through to the waiting lounge.

Once the test samples were taken, the nurse told them, "Your results should be available on Tuesday mid-morning, so would you want to come and collect them in person, rather than waiting for the mail? We can let you know by SMS or email."

"Absolutely - we both can't wait to find out!" When they were all through, they came out into a brighter street, as the sun had come out - almost like a reflection of what they'd just gone through. Andy suggested they get a bagel or something from a diner nearby, and tak a picnic lunch into the sunshine in Central Park.

On the walk to the park, they shared more about their work and their lives and realised there were more similarities that kept coming up - not least that they were both still single. Not for lack of trying for either of them. "I've dated and Tindered and whatever," Gino sighed "I just never really clicked with anyone - not someone to think about sharing a life with."

Andy nodded, "Same. And I've worked at it believe me, even going as far as getting engaged. That was a couple of years ago now, and then the relationship just drifted. I just didn't feel it, I think and it felt like a dead end. I thought that maybe coming over to the US would let me make that clean break."

"I get that - a new start, but that's some break, man."

"I know, but I was a bit at sea. Maybe I thought that being a Brit may give me an edge in finding the right person, but - it's certainly not worked so far. Maybe I don't even know what I'm looking for. I've met a few women I've liked but not really gone beyond that first step. And I was right, being a Brit obviously doesn't hinder that first date - as I'm - well, we're both pretty good looking guys!"

Entering the park, they took a moment and followed the path to the Conservatory Pond, just inside the park. There were a few others enjoying a relaxed lunch looking out over the water, in the late spring sunshine and they found a bench to sit. A couple of retired guys were on the far side by the boathouse, launching a radio control model sailboat. The boys watched as they pushed it away from the shore, and it eased away across the water under a light breeze.

"Max has this thing about me and Michelle being a good match - and I've been out on dates with her a few times, movies, lunch and whatever. She's a good friend but I can't really go beyond that with her. We kinda, 'friend zoned' too early on. And like us she's still unattached - we're like some kinda sad singles club!"

"I was wondering who Michelle was," Gino looked puzzled at him, "Max had said something about Michelle coming along, when he saw me at Bryant Park that first morning - after mistaking me for you! I heard him say something about her later that evening too. That all makes sense now."

"Yeah, she's Max's ex-colleague from his real estate business, we've known each other for years now. You're going to have to meet her, she's one of the team. They still do similar kinds of work, but they're both more into the commercial side - plush office suites, you know the kind of thing."

"Got it, that makes sense. I understand why he mentioned her now."

They watched together as the sailboat on the pond was being carried by a gust of breeze towards them, nearing the edge of the pond, and then turned around and started tacking into the wind. Gino pointed, "that's us now, man. Looks like our lives may well be changing course," he laughed.

"Hah, very poetic. But you're probably not far wrong."

"I'm gonna go over to Mom's house tomorrow and help her go through some more of the files and boxes of old documents from the attic. She said there could be things she'd not seen for years, as long as it's all still there. She'll do me a good lunch as well, which is always a bonus - she's an amazing home cook."

They parted after their picnic to get back to their offices - with a wait stretching ahead for the DNA results to come.

It was a strange transition time, Andy was thinking. Clearly, they must be connected - but without the confirmation of a test result, he felt it was still up in the air. Like he was almost holding his breath.

He slipped back into his familiar life in Queens that evening with a quick gym session before heading to the bar for a few beers with a friend who lived nearby, then watching the Chelsea league match against Everton on the Saturday morning, back in Manhattan. He'd meet up with other ex-pat Chelsea fans he'd come across at the Chelsea supporters' home bar of course, all wanting to see if the blues could win with a clean sheet for the first time in ages.

He couldn't share it of course, but almost like a constant backdrop, dominating the back of his mind, there was Gino, and the clock ticking on waiting for the DNA results next week.

He was going to call as soon as he heard anything from the clinic - this could well change both their lives and their families.

— **7** —

Tuesday - results

Tuesday, just as the nurse at the clinic had told them, Gino had had the text from the clinic to say the DNA test results were available to collect by hand and phoned first thing to arrange the time. He planned his day around it, before meeting Andy again for lunch. They'd decided they wanted to open the results envelope together, so both made their ways towards the Canaletto restaurant in mid-town to meet up.

The Canaletto was a small Italian, just off 3rd Avenue, and Gino was sat at an outside table, not in his usual sharp suit, but more casual. "Hey Andy, how's it going? I chose this as it's a bit quieter around here, and about half way between us - I'm working on a quick refurb between renters on the upper East Side this week. So, no client facing," as he gestured to his casual appearance.

"Going well?" Andy asked, as he sat down opposite, "Yeah it is. But, far more important, I guess - this is the moment of truth!" as he held the envelope up.

Gino opened it, then handed it to Andy. Pulling out the sheets of paper, as they moved the glasses and pepper mill, they spread the papers across the tablecloth to read it together.

'Based on the analysis of 21 genetic markers, the probability of the two samples provided being related is 100%. The genetic profiles appear to be 99% identical. We would expect that the two samples to be from genetically identical twins.'

Gino looked up from the letter, smiled and uttered a gentle "whoa, whoa, whoa! So - that sounds like… pretty conclusive to me - my dear twin brother Andrew!", he smiled, shaking his head.

"It certainly does. Well - and here's a hello to my twin brother Gino!" They looked at each other, made for a formal handshake, and just laughed, loud enough so other diners turned and looked. "Wow - that - makes… you know, we both knew it was coming, as it's plain as day."

"100% Andy - whew! As Mom said, it was 'plain as the noses on your faces'. But seeing it there in black and white…" Gino toyed with his pasta, looking again at the print out, "changes things a lot - doesn't it?"

"Yep. Watching the match at the weekend, I was thinking I was in like a limbo before it was confirmed. I've been trying to think how to make that change in who I think I am - I'm now half of a pair of twins. Always was, but didn't know it! The way we both see ourselves will have to be different. I'm not just one bloke anymore… but I don't really know how I should feel."

"Changing course like that sailboat, eh?" he laughed.

"Hah, you're right. And the nurse did stress that the familial test is highly accurate as well - 99% looks conclusive to me. More so than the online family history ones."

"I get what you mean - our worlds have both just shifted. And I've been reading up a bit about a special bond between twins - but would that be because they usually grow up together or…"

"…is it something almost there by instinct… I guess that we may well find out," Andy smiled, as they clinked glasses, "Cheers - and here's to finding out."

Gino looked thoughtful as he ate, "You know, I said when I was younger, I'd always wanted a brother. Mom always said that too, as you know but that didn't happen. But for her, she always said it was more for me to have someone to play ball with. But for me, I don't think that was in the way you sometimes hear about separated twins, who always knew something was missing - like there was a gap, I'm not sure there was. But maybe that could be why I connected so well with Max, when we were very young. He was an only child too, and always around our place."

"That makes sense,"

Gino paused, "But… maybe there could be something in those stories about separation, where they say they always knew they were a missing twin. It's gotten me thinking about what I felt as a kid. Not sure how - thinking back I can't think of how that should have felt. One thing's for sure; it's going to take some getting used to now."

Andy agreed, "Too true. I was lucky I suppose. Like I said the other day, when they got me, Mum reckoned that adopting me removed the stress of trying too hard to have a baby, then Leon came. So, I had a younger brother to play football with, and go out on our bikes to the park, but he was quite a bit younger."

Gino looked thoughtful, "The bit she said about the test being more accurate than online ones, that got me thinking about... about family history I guess, and where I - we came from. This test is a stand alone - and just confirms us as being… well, us," Gino paused, "but it has set me off thinking about the poor woman - or girl, who gave birth to us both in Dublin. Was she an unmarried mother, or what?"

"That would still have been pretty much frowned on in Ireland in the 70's, and even the 80's, or maybe she was in a situation where she just couldn't cope with twins. But you're right, she must have wondered what happened to us. It would be interesting to find out more, I suppose."

Gino pushed his empty plate away, "When Mom and I went through the documents at the weekend, we found some important information in the adoption file. I told you the name of my birth Mom was shown as the same as the one your mom said - Brenda Kelly."

Andy laughed, "So that's pretty clear, and that name will be fun to chase down - a bit like John Smith in England. There must be hundreds and maybe thousands of Brenda Kellys in Ireland - and in the rest of Britain even."

"I know what they were saying about online tests not being as accurate, but there must be something in it. Perhaps we should look at one of those online family history searches with an online DNA test. It could sure help us find a cousin, or brother, whatever - who knows, maybe even our birth mother?"

"I'd be happy to give it a try if you are bro."

"I sure am, *bro*! It sounds like both our moms are as bought in as we are to all this. This is likely to be emotionally tricky to tackle - so we better make sure they're OK with us taking this next step. If she's OK and your mom - 'mum', is OK with it, then we should do it. I'll call mom after lunch and let her know the test results, though she's already convinced we're twins."

"Makes sense. You're right, I need to speak to my mum. I'll see if she's around when I get back home and give her the news and bring up the idea of searching for the birth family at the same time. I'd hate them to feel like being… sidelined maybe, or left out certainly, and let you know what she says. If both our mothers are OK with it, we can start the ball rolling."

"OK, and in that case, who's going to do it? Your turn?" asked Gino, "I'm sure genetically speaking, we don't both need to do it!"

"Sure thing, and it would be simpler with just one of us - we'll not need to find each other now. I can check out the options. I know there are at least a couple of big ones, so probably best to use the one that has the best Irish connections; I'll take a look at the reviews and compare the details. I could get signed up anyway to find out how long it all takes; will probably be a few weeks - it can't be as quick as the clinic was."

The two brothers headed back to work for the afternoon. Andy phoned his mum on the way back to the office, to let her know the DNA test results. "I had no doubt at all Andrew, from what you've been telling me, and from that photo."

"This has all got both of us thinking about the woman who gave birth to us. She may not want to know about us, but could have lived a whole life just wondering what became of us. We were wondering if you'd be OK with us taking the step, and doing an online Ancestry test, like on the TV shows."

"That is so thoughtful of you both - I guess we did both a decent job of bringing you up. I'd have no problem at all, as long as Gino's mum feels the same. And I can only imagine, if that girl Brenda was forced to give you up, what she must have been going through, probably all her life."

"That's great Mum - we'll get started looking at that. I'll call again tomorrow, and bring you up to speed properly, if that's OK. I need to get back to work."

Back in the studio, Andy gave Denny his DNA news, "So mate. Bombshell here - we were 99% identical according to the test results and conclusively identical twins."

"I just knew it, bud!"

"And the latest on the family saga is that we're thinking of doing one of the family history tests. We're both thinking that there's a woman somewhere, who's wondered what happened to us, for over 40 years - or if not, we may have other relations, who knows."

Denny laughed, "This is just wild Andy, it feels like I'm an extra in some kind of old time soap opera - or maybe that podcast idea!"

Andy messaged Gino to let him know his mum can't wait to find out more. Gino came back to him, saying that his mom Angie was really positive, and encouraged them to do it as well.

He went online to find out more about the family history testing. It seemed that Ancestry and FindMyPast were both pretty strong for Ireland, and he picked the first mainly because it was the most used from what reviewers and a couple of Subreddits had advised. They could always switch to the other one if they drew a blank.

He signed up online, and ordered the Ancestry DNA test kit; then messaged Gino that he'd found that it would take a few days to arrive, and the results anything from a couple of weeks after sending the sample in.

He sat back… and was still mentally pinching himself that this was all real. It was so hard to believe that it was still just a week since they first came across each other in Dillon's bar - and he saw his own likeness walking towards him. It really was the strangest experience, looking back at it. They really couldn't thank Max enough for mistaking him that morning in Bryant Park.

Given the speed that all this had come at them so far, it felt like way more than a week; he was finding it hard to come to terms with the fact that they'll just have to be patient for the next stage. He had to wait for the kit to arrive - and even then, it was going to be a few weeks til anything came back from Ancestry. Andy called Gino to see if he fancied a beer one evening - "the Irish bar maybe?"

"Sure, I've nothing planned tomorrow if that works. About 6ish?"

— 8 —

Wednesday beers

They met at the same barrel table in Dillon's bar. Gino ordered a beer and a Guinness for Andy, and shared that had been reading up a bit about twins separated at birth on Reddit and a few personal experience blogs.

"I know it's not gospel truth on these sites, but one of the things that stuck in my head after reading one personal story on Reddit was that even before birth - how'd they put it…" he opened Notes on his phone, "yeah, this is it: 'twins form a primary attachment to each other in the womb. When this bond is broken at birth, it can leave a deep sense of loss and emptiness that can carry through into adult life.' That really made me think. Even asked myself if it's something I've experienced. Not that I can say if I'm honest."

"Oh wow, not sure I've felt that - loss and emptiness - either. But there may be something in it… and I suppose it's not surprising that we have both had issues building relationships."

"I guess," said Gino, "Makes sense. It went on to say: 'When separated at birth, twins may look for this same kind of deep understanding in other relationships - and be disappointed with non-twin partners or friends.' …which kinda makes a lot of sense - just like you said. Though I've always felt close to Max… maybe I was latching on to him as a replacement twin," he laughed, "I'll see if I can find that link and send it to you."

"Thanks, I could do with reading about it all myself I suppose. It's not something I'd even thought about before last week! But it sounds like it's going to be useful to understand myself - ourselves - a bit better," Andy smiled.

"Also, Mom asked if you'd like to come for lunch on Sunday at her place out on the Island - now that you're 'family'. We can take the LI double-R out to Glen Cove, or we can UBER it. She said she'd do a Pork shoulder and 'Sunday gravy' - now *that* is something special. You'll love it."

"Sounds very interesting! I'd love to come - it will be great to meet her. It will make a welcome change to watching the Chelsea match - maybe if I'm not watching it they'll win for a change," he laughed.

"Not been a good season for them?"

"Mixed - as usual, despite the expensive new signings last January."

Gino said he was planning to take a look through some of the old family photos as well while they were there to share. It would be interesting to find out if there are more similarities when they were growing up.

The Stone Roses song 'I wanna be adored' had just started playing over the sound system - and Andy sang along with the chorus when it came around, "One of my favourite bands, this."

"Don't think I know much about them Andy, must be a Brit thing."

"Could be, I suppose. They're part of the Manc scene coming out of the Hacienda club - you'll probably have come across Happy Mondays, Chemical Brothers, Oasis?"

"Yeah - maybe from coming in here with Max and his crew - this is a pretty Brit place with all these 'Toon Army' banners and soccer matches on the TV."

"My brother Leon was more into the Hip Hop scene - loved Dizzee Rascal and Tinie Tempah and all that stuff. But he mixed with a different crowd at school anyway - I was very much 'the white boy with red hair'." he smiled.

"How d'you mean?"

Andy realised he'd not mentioned it before. "I mentioned Leon was born a few years after I was adopted, didn't I?" Gino nodded, "Mum had given up on trying for a baby before I came on the scene. From then on, she supposed that the pressure was off - and then it just happened. My Dad's family is actually from Barbados - so Leon looked a lot more like my dad. Living in Brixton, he fitted in better at school; there's a very strong Caribbean community around there. There you go, here's a photo of him…"

"Wow, I see what you mean. So your brother's called Leon?"

Andy brought up another photo of Leon with their mum from last Christmas and a couple more from further back; one of the two of them when they were younger and a photo of Mum and Dad together.

"I guess that must have made life interesting! Caribbean dad and strawberry blond mom. It makes sense that you settled in Queens. Now there's a melting pot."

They talked more about their musical lives. Andy shared his listening, "I love some of the jazz and Caribbean sounds I grew up with - mostly from Dad. He loved Barbados 'Bajan spouge' which no-one's ever heard about and 'reggae' of course. I've been getting into the current jazz guitar scene too. And I like some of the newer crop of singer songwriters, like Adele and Ed Sheeran are pretty good. I guess I'm getting old. Tends to be Bach or Debussy working in the studio - lyrics tend to cut into thinking about the job in hand."

Gino's music growing up was a mix as well. His Dad loved Sinatra and all that Rat Pack stuff, as well as the jazz greats, Oscar Peterson and Ellington, "Mom likes that too but really loves the Motown disco sounds! You may find out how much on Sunday!"

"It struck me a while back, thinking about Leon, how much our music choices are shaped by the people around us. You know, parents' music, like both of us and the friends we choose or connect with. Suppose it could work both ways - you connect with people who share your taste in music."

Gino agreed, "I get that - could go either way - Max and I used to go to his place and listen to some of his CDs and we really got into bands like Aerosmith, Maroon 5 type stuff," he looked thoughtful, "Dad's old school jazz is still fun to listen to - but I guess that could be the nostalgia kicking in? I'm not into classical at all, really. There's tunes I like, but couldn't tell you what they are or sit through a concert!"

They shared some of the gigs they'd been to, "the most exciting for me was Glastonbury in 2003, I think it was. I went with a few friends from Art College - along with over 100,000 other people."

"Wow - yeah, I've heard of it. Sounds amazing and I've seen some YouTubes from it. Who did you get to see?"

"Some amazing bands - I guess REM and Radiohead were great - but I loved the Waterboys and Sigur Ros too and quite a lot of others I'd never heard of too. It's so immersive - it's like a whole town, with lots of different themed stages and music genres. Almost too much maybe - but totally amazing."

They talked music for a while over a few beers and a lot more conversation, catching up on 40 years of lives led separately before calling it a night.

"I'll pick you up in an UBER around 11 on Sunday and we can head up to Mom's place - she really can't wait to meet you, man. This is going to be… I dunno - strange maybe. Anyhow, we'll see, I'm sure."

"I get what you mean - I'm sure it will be fine. Your mum sounds OK - and it will be nice to explore a bit of Long Island as well," he waved as they both headed for the subway.

Sunday sounded like it could turn out to be interesting, Andy thought to himself, 'Now you're family' Gino had said. Now, there's an interesting concept he thought, "I still can't quite wrap my head around it all, being an identical twin and all that goes with it. I'll drop Mum a note and let her know I'm going to meet his mom."

He settled back into the podcast, as the subway passed under the East River, heading home.

Andy called his mum the next morning to keep her up to date. He told her that Gino would love to meet her when she comes over - and maybe she'd like to meet his mom Angie as well. He talked through what the DNA results showed with her and what that meant for them both, "and Gino said his mom has asked me to Sunday Lunch this weekend. It seems she's an amazing cook, so I can't wait to find out for myself."

"That will be lovely for you - and I'm jealous, she'll get to see the two of you side by side before me!"

"There's been a few who've beaten you to that - Gino's friend Max, and of course Denny from the office, we've become pretty good friends in recent months. I'll call Leon as well, and see how he's fixed to come over with you - and I'll bring Dad up to speed on our news. This has all happened so fast Mum, it's hard to believe."

"It does seem like only yesterday - an awful lot's changed for you in just a week."

"And I'm not sure how to think about it all. Gino and I were talking yesterday when we picked up the results, and he's thinking the same as me. We've been reading how twins can have an almost instinctive bond, but neither of us think we've ever felt that. We've found some more similarities between us as well - both still single, despite wanting to have a steady relationship - and probably more we'll find out in the next few weeks."

"I'm sure you will, and it sounds as though you two have developed a bit of a friendship already. And let me know what Gino's mum says about meeting her when we come over."

"Will do. I've got to head to the office now so, speak to you soon Mum."

— **9** —

Sunday at Mom's

Gino's UBER pulled up outside Andy's place just before 11, to head out east onto Long Island and up to Glen Cove, "beautiful flowers, man - for me?" he smiled.

Andy laughed, "Well, when visiting a lady of a certain age, flowers are usually a good bet to get on their good side."

"I'm sure you'll have no problem doing that man - after all we're not that different. But yeah, she'll love them. She loves her backyard and growing veggies in the garden and all that."

They chatted as the cab took them way out past Manhasset and Roslyn, then past a sea inlet out to the left of the main road. They turned to the North soon after that, towards Glen Cove, then off into the Sea Cliff area.

Andy hadn't really been out to Long Island much since arriving in New York, apart from a trip last summer out to Coopers Beach near Southampton. He'd usually gone by train and cab, and never really considered buying a car since moving to New York - parking would have been difficult in Woodside and it would be madness to drive into Manhattan - driving often takes twice as long as the subway.

Most of the friends he'd made and things he went to were based around Queens or back in Manhattan and just like a lot of his friends, Zipcar was the obvious choice for occasional trips, or rental if you need something bigger.

As they turned off into the Glen Cove area, it almost felt like a British town or village in places - though the houses were of course very different, as they drove through a maze of very pretty but narrow hilly streets.

Gino pointed out some of the local sights, and they caught a glimpse of the bay through the trees to the North as they rounded a bend downhill and shortly afterwards came to a stop. Gino's mom lived in a lovely looking grey painted traditional wood house (a bit like the clapboard ones on the Essex coast) on a fair size plot, with a traditional porch right across the front. There was even a rocking chair on one side. It had obviously had a lot of love lavished on it - and so had the garden, with mature shrubs along the path to the door.

Mrs Bianchi greeted them at the front door. "Oh my! There can be no mistake - you must be Andy - though I'll bet your mom calls you Andrew?"

"Absolutely she does, Mrs. Bia…"

"Do call me Angie,' she cut in, "I still keep looking round for Joe's mom if I hear 'Mrs. Bianchi'! How interesting that you both had an adopted father called Joseph." She stopped and looked at them both, "You two really are so alike it's so unreal, even more than that photo. I'm just glad that at least your hair is a different length! Oh, listen to me jabbering! Come along inside, Andy. Should I guess that bouquet is for me?"

"Of course, it's the least I could do.

"He's keen to get on your good side Mom."

"Ha ha, he'll not need to do anything apart from be himself, I'm sure. I've prepared some coffee - or would you prefer tea?"

"Coffee would be great Mrs… Angie. I'll get used to calling you that, I'm sure." They followed her into the house and sat at the kitchen island to talk while coffee brewed, with Marvin Gaye playing in the background. The smell of the Sunday lunch cooking was almost overwhelming. "That smells absolutely amazing, Gino warned me that your cooking is legendary."

"Aw, go on with you - it's just good old Italian family food." She almost blushed, "It's all about taking the time, and adding just enough love into it."

They took their coffees to sit outside on the terrace, "anyways, I want to hear all the details again, about how you two met and everything. Gino was telling me all about how Max mistook you from across the street - and that doesn't surprise me, not in the least." Andy told Angie the story as he'd seen it unfold in Bryant Park, and then in the bar 'later' and the two of them laughed as they recounted Max's expression when they met, "that was quite something, eh Gino, his face was like something from Tom & Jerry."

"Now, Gino's told me a little bit about your mother - Jeannette isn't it? …and your brother Leon?"

"Yes, he did." Andy shared some more of his background, growing up in South London and his design career, "that was what brought me to New York. And of course, we'd probably never have discovered each other, had it not been for Max spotting me. That really had me confused for that whole Tuesday until they rolled into the bar later that day."

They talked more about that strange meeting, and the thoughts they'd both been having about it all. They both shared how it was such a change trying to understand their feelings since finding out 100% sure that they are twin brothers. Gino shared, "I think it has almost changed my perspective on life. Not taking away from everything you do, Mom."

"I know what you mean Gino, I've been thinking about all this a lot since we talked about it the other day, it's like another door has opened almost. We've both had great family upbringings - but like we've both said, there's some poor woman probably in Ireland still, and maybe in Dublin who's been wondering for 40 or so years about what happened to us."

They talked through the Ancestry process they'd set going with Angie in more detail, and how Andy had sent off the sample just on Thursday, "so if it takes seven to ten days, then we've a wait ahead of us."

"Yeah Mom, so we may find out more soon after - that's assuming that there's someone else out there who's also done the DNA test - and maybe knows about us already."

"This all feels just like we're living through one of those lost family TV programmes," said Andy, smiling as they moved back into the kitchen.

Angie agreed "I know, it really does! Oh, and I just love watching your British 'Long Lost Family' TV show on PBS. It's like a beautiful slice of someone else's life, and that Nicky guy is just, ooh!" she smiled with a bit of a twinkle.

She paused to stir the pan on the stove top, "Hmm… dear Max really started something here, didn't he? And, you know what, I'm really interested that you're both involved in something creative, you as a designer and Gino here in interior design. I wonder if this creative side comes from your genes - it's not come from me or your Pa."

"Nor on my side Angie. Dad was a train driver and Mum a nurse."

"Hmm," Gino mused, "you always wonder if that kind of thing is nature or nurture. Like, musicians often come from a family where they all play instruments, like the Bachs - or Loudon Wainwright's family maybe."

"Or my favourites, Nat and Natalie Cole, I see what you mean." thought Angie, "well, lunch should be about ready now. The fettucini feels about there now. Gino can you fix some salad for the main, while I dish up the Primo. Andy, I hope you like my cooking - after everything Gino's said to raise your expectations," she smiled as she placed their dishes in front of them.

Andy sat at the table and took in the aroma of tomatoes, rosemary and basil, as Angie put his dish in front of him, "Wow - so that's the 'Sunday Gravy' you mentioned? It smells amazing. How does the flavour get so intense?"

"Andy, that will have been cooking around the pork for hours man, a real Italian tradition."

"So, a bigger job than a simple bolognese then?"

"Oh yes, it's been simmering away for about 4-5 hours Andy! It's pretty much the same recipe my Momma used - and probably her Momma before her back in Calabria. It's all about good honest ingredients - not necessarily the best piece of meat - oh but really good tomatoes - as it cooks right down and sits bubbling away on the stove top thickening all the time. Don't be mistaken, even a simple Bolognese should cook for a long time as well to bring the full flavour out."

After the pasta course, the Secundo truly delivered what the 'Sunday Gravy' had promised. Rich tender pork that melted into the sauce of tomatoes and red bell peppers, "I think I really missed out on the food stakes, being brought up in South London! Though we love Grandma's cooking that she'd brought over from Barbados."

"So, it wasn't all Roast Beef dinners and fish & chips then, Andy?"

"English food isn't as bad as it's billed Gino. My Mum still cooks some of those dishes. Grandma bemoaned that she couldn't get the flying fish like they used back home for the Cou Cou, which is like cornmeal and Okra. The Pepper Pot was my favourite with beef and oxtail and lots of Scotch Bonnet chillies."

"That sounds like it would pack quite some punch," Angie laughed, "I guess there's a mix of all the people from across the old Empire living in Britain now, and a lot of different styles - I've read about how curries are the most popular take out food over there."

"Yes exactly Angie, Chicken Tikka Masala is effectively Britain's favourite dish - and I think that was invented in Birmingham or Glasgow or somewhere. But even Fish & Chips isn't English - that was brought in by the Yiddish immigrants from Eastern Europe, I think."

"Sure is similar to here, we brought the pasta and Italian food over from Calabria, there's bagels and Lox in Manhattan, Chinatown, like the one in San Francisco Joe took me to and plenty more here in the US. It will be great to see your mom as well, like Gino mentioned if she decides to come over."

As they relaxed over coffee, Gino dug out some of the older family photos to show Andy. "This one reminds me a bit of the one you showed me of you and Leon,"

"Yes, I see what you mean. It's like we were in parallel universes. Oh, and that's a young Max - without a moustache?"

"Yep, and my Pop, there in the background with the catcher's glove. Oh, by the way I was thinking we should arrange to meet up with Max and Denny again on the Tuesday evening in Dillon's - like a '2-weekiversary' or something,"

"Hey, that sounds a fun idea; he seems a really nice guy. I'll get Denny along too - get the team back together."

Heading back home after a richly rewarding day, Andy felt as though they'd really managed to come together and it all just seemed… natural - in such a short time. The two brothers sat back in the cab and mulled over everything they'd talked about during the day with Angie, "and Mom's amazing food!"

"I think one of the really fascinating things that hit me today," Andy mused, "was despite knowing each other for less than two weeks, how we just - get along. Do you know what I mean?"

"I'd not really thought about it - just accepted it I guess. But yeah… that's it."

"Maybe there's something in all this about the special twin relationship. I mean, Leon and I get on but there's always that something - sibling rivalry - competition - whatever it is."

"That's where you have the edge - I never had any of that. Max is the nearest I had to that kind of relationship - and yeah like all kids we argued a bit but I guess without the family bit. My cousins were not around much and always felt more - kinda formal almost. We don't live close - My mom's sister moved out to Jersey. And Dad's sister married into the military, so they moved around the bases. And, by the way, I let Max know about our results - I guess that's cool?"

"I've been keeping Denny up to date as well - he calls it the 'missing twins podcast' or something. I wonder what other family we'll discover - if we do actually find any. This next bit of this journey should be interesting - and completely uncharted."

The brothers parted as they reached Andy's apartment. "So, we're meeting up with Max again on Tuesday? So, I'll see you then - unless I get a really quick response from Ancestry!" Gino waved from the window as the cab pulled away.

Mom's thoughts

"Oh my, what a lovely guy Andy is - well he would be wouldn't he! And it's so good he appreciates good home cooking. His mother Jeannette

sounds lovely from what he said about her, and we have had such a parallel experience.

"I really can't believe that that agency hadn't even told us about Andy - what kind of person splits up twins? That really hurts - I'm sure we'd have taken both boys - but I guess so would Jeannette. And after all, we only went along with the idea of the Dublin agency to avoid that 'Baby Scoop' corruption going on at the time in New York - our priest's idea would you believe!

"I wonder if Andy's mother really is thinking of coming over. Though he said he just saw her a couple of months ago - but this is… Hey, I know I would be too curious to see them both together to miss the chance.

"And this Ancestry thing the boys are talking about has gotten me thinking about their birth mother again. I'd sort of buried that deep down. The poor woman, fancy not knowing anything about them for all these years. My heart goes out - really goes out to her - it always did as I'd always light a candle to pray for her every year. Without her, I'd not have had Gino in my life - or now these twins!!

"Hey, well, let's see what this next bit of the story brings along."

—— **10** ——

Tuesday, 2 weeks in

Andy and Gino arrived early after work at Dillon's within minutes of each other, to celebrate their 'two weekiversary' of having met up for the first time in over 40 years! Gino had a beer ready for each of them, and they chatted together about their day's work and the similar challenges they face in their creative lives.

Gino asked how designers were coping with everything being online, "I mean years ago you could see all the magazine adverts and printed brochures - now I'd guess everything's online and keeps changing, yeah?"

"Yes, a lot's changed since I first started in graphic design. It used to be all brochures and mailers printed from manually planned colour separations. We still print stuff of course but we designers get involved in a wider range of projects - so we're always learning new software. Every website needs designing, so that's a whole new area of design which didn't exist before. And in my own area, stuff still needs packaging - even when it's sold online. And when it's instore, they need shelf barkers, outers and point of sale materials."

"I guess you're right. We're in a much more designed world I guess."

"...and the technology has made things so much easier. Easier to make quick ad hoc design changes. Years ago, planning the artwork and film separations would have taken a team of guys a week to get to print. Now our graphics package just outputs directly to the printing plates."

"And AI can make some stuff happen without us getting involved!" Gino laughed. "At least in interior design, stuff still needs to be built and remodeled. Like yours, our design packages make life so much simpler, but someone has to build the furnishings. Ah, here comes Max… oh, and Denny."

Max joked "It's almost like we're here for a 'return fixture' as they say," looking up at the Newcastle match on the TV above the bar.

"This time Gino, I've made sure Michelle's gonna be coming along after work. I told her a little bit about you finding someone called Andy who looks like you - but left it at that. She sounded intrigued - a bit left out of the loop - a bit of FOMO should bring her running!" he said with a grin.

"Jeez, Max. That's just cruel! So she doesn't know anything about Andy?"

"Just his name. I wanted her to have the same experience we all did," smiled Max.

"You should have let us know - he could have had a hair cut in the same style," Denny laughed.

The new found twins brought Max and Denny up to speed with everything that had happened over the last week. They both already knew about the results from the first DNA test, of course, and shared what their two mothers - Mum and Mom - had been saying about taking the search further to look for their birth mother.

"So, neither of them were upset by it? I guess I'd been thinking that they might see it as disloyal with you both going off looking for her."

"That's what we were worried about, but not a bit of it, Max. They're both right behind us aren't they Andy - and wanting us to let Brenda know that we're both alive and well,"

"Yeah - both of them were appalled that we'd been split up and I suppose, want us to try and find her - though we're assuming she wants to be found…"

A voice rang out as they were talking, "Hey Max, Gino, so what's all this about? Max has been so cage…" She stopped short, as she looked first at Andy and back at Gino - several times. "What the…?"

The group burst into laughter, "haha, that's just what we all first said, Michelle." said Max, still laughing, "I just wanted you to get the same experience we all had two weeks ago."

"So, this is the Andy you mentioned - and you kept this 'little detail' to yourself? How have you not told me about Andy before? You knew each other before?" Gino shook his head about to reply, "...then how did this happen? How long have you guys known each other?"

"Sorry for the shock - all Max's idea. It was a totally chance meeting. I first saw Andy just two weeks ago - about this time - walking into this bar, like you just did. We both just stopped and looked at each other! The past two weeks have been some breakneck ride, with us both finding out a whole lot more about ourselves!"

Gino and Andy shared the whole story so far with Michelle - the meeting, the DNA test and everything - while she sat open-mouthed, looking at them both. "This really is like one of those TV dramas - like that one about 3 identical strangers. Hey, I hope there's not another one of you hiding somewhere, is there?" She was obviously really hooked by the story, as Denny came back into the group. "And who's this? - at least you don't look the same, thank God!"

"Michelle, meet Denny - my friend and colleague." said Andy, "I know what you mean about the TV show, my Mum watches the family history programmes on TV in Britain - almost religiously. She'll not miss an episode."

"Yeah, same here. Mom was telling us both at the weekend, she loves those shows and doesn't miss. I guess it's understandable, as I was adopted. And now we're giving them their very own personalised episode, Andy!"

Michelle laughed, "Jeez, I'm still trying to catch up in my head - this is just so... so," she took a moment to catch her thoughts," So, OK, you did a DNA test that proved you are genetically the same - so actual - full on - twins. Holy shit, guys - that's just wild! How'd that happen?"

"Yes, this has been an interesting couple of weeks, and as Gino said, I've met his mom already," Andy smiled, "turns out we were both adopted from the same place in Ireland. And we're about to go another step, and do an Ancestry test as well."

"Oh wow, and I'm guessing you're from the UK Andy?"

Andy nodded, "which partly explains why we knew nothing about each other."

"So, why do you need that, if the DNA test was so sure?"

"Well, we got to thinking about who gave birth to us. We know from both of our adoption papers that it was someone called Brenda Kelly in Dublin, Ireland. The next step could help us see where we actually came from, and hopefully find some relatives - maybe even find our birth mother." Andy went on, in a more muted tone, "So we know the name of the woman or girl who gave birth to us, but the names Brenda or Kelly aren't that unusual over there!"

Gino continued, "...and she may have spent four decades not knowing what happened to her babies. This Ancestry test will show anyone else with shared DNA connections, anywhere in the world - so long as they've taken a test. So - no idea what we'll find, but we guess it's worth giving it a whirl."

Michelle nodded, "I get it. I recently found out my grandma had a baby girl adopted when she was young, before she was married, and my mom has been trying to trace her... her half-sibling - she's using a different website though I think."

"Oh wow, I didn't know about that. Andy's done a bit of research and Ancestry should be a good fit for us, as they have a strong Irish database. We've no idea what we'll dig up. It may be that we were a family secret, the mother may have been unmarried and thrown out because of the pregnancy,"

Andy nodded, "...or it could have been she was just unable to bring us up and handed us to the nuns in Dublin. We've no idea what we'll find, and not sure if it will clear up why we were separated."

"Oh, I get that, it could be really interesting - and may turn out pretty emotional I guess." Michelle truly 'got it', "I can't imagine going through two births - well I can't imagine that part anyway," she laughed, "and then probably only see your two babies for hours or a few weeks at most."

"There is the possibility of course," Andy continued, "that she won't want to open old wounds, after all this time. Or she may well have died and buried the secret. Whatever it is, this is going to rustle some feathers, probably..."

"We could be setting a bomb off in what they know about their family." Gino finished.

"Oh jeez... I get that. Are you sure about what you're doing?" she asked.

"Not totally - but we both think we have to do it." Andy answered. "What if she's been marking every birthday and wondering? We've got to give her the chance to know what happened to us."

"Even if it's just to let her know that we both had great adoptions and a good life," Gino added, "sometimes that can be enough."

"Oh wow, can you two hear yourselves?" Michelle asked, "it's like you're finishing each others' sentences - and the same kind of rhythm. Surely that is just so weird given how long you've known each other?"

"100%, I was just thinking the same," agreed Denny, who'd just been taking it all in from the sidelines, "you guys are so in sync - it's like hearing a Jazz duet. It's getting hard to keep up with them."

"I suppose it must be inevitable - but maybe that it's just because we're both so involved in this same situation - from an 'identical' viewpoint really," Andy explained, "and we've met up a few times already, and spoken on the phone to keep up with things."

"...and, yeah Andy's right. We really are - it's almost like we're both in the same place. You're right though Michelle; it is a bit weird when you think about it!"

"Gino - you've spoken on the phone?" asked Max, "You never - or rarely call me - it's always a text or WhatsApp."

"Yeah, yeah, I know - anyhow we spoke just the other day!"

"I called you, man! I stand by it, you 'never call me'," Max laughed.

"It's usually easier, at least I reach you that way. Like I said we're in some kind of a twilight zone. There's been too much to discuss - hey we've got 40 years to catch up on - and a family to find!"

The group of friends - and new friends shared the stories they'd heard from others, their own experiences - and their thoughts on how this family history search might go. Who they might find and what kind of hornets nest they are about to poke.

Michelle had seen some of the lost family reunion TV shows and agreed that this could go either way. She had a friend who went through a similar process recently, so had some idea of how the story could go. She was caught up in trying to imagine what it must be like, "How tough must it be to give up a child that had been growing inside you for nine months, plus all the pain of childbirth - let alone to give up two perfect twins."

"Aww, Michelle, perfect twins? How sweet!" Gino laughed.

"Well, you probably were back then," laughed Michelle, "though I guess you've not lost too much of your shine boys!"

"Well, all that being said," Andy added, "we might be closer to finding something out sometime soon - I'm waiting for results to appear in the app. That's assuming, as Gino said, that anyone else we're potentially related to has done a test in the same app. If that doesn't come up with anything, then there are a couple of other websites to try out - they're not connected to each others' data, so this may take a while."

"It's felt like forever already since you sent the test sample off, Andy. But yeah - it's something we really both need to know now."

"I hope you boys'll keep us all updated on the latest news," Denny said, looking at Michelle and Max. "We all want to hear the next instalment - of the 'Missing Twins Podcast'!"

"I like it. Though it's more like that 'Long Lost Family' show!" Max laughed.

The evening ended on a very relaxed note, with the friends separating to head for their subways homeward.

— **11** —

Another Thursday

Andy woke with a start - with a notification on his phone from the Ancestry app. He hesitated, and sat up looking at the screen - from deep sleep to wide awake in just a few seconds.

He hesitated. This was too momentous a thing to do on a phone app, so got himself moving and went through to switch the kettle on and logged into the website on his laptop. Yep, the 'notifications' bell icon was lit up. He messaged Gino to let him know the results were in. He suggested a breakfast call after his shower.

Cup of tea in hand, he sent a Zoom link over, so they could both see whatever the message was. Gino appeared in the window as Andy sat back at the table, looking a bit more awake than Andy, "Good morning, bro! Looks like we've hooked a connection. OK, I'll share my screen so you can see what I see."

He clicked on the account, a graph showed over 80% of DNA as being from Ireland and some in England and one in Australia. Nothing in the US which he thought was unusual, "so many Irish ended up in the US, it seems odd that there's nothing showing."

"Yeah - but that all makes sense I guess," Gino said. "Listen, I'm running a bit late and have to head out to an early meeting now. Can we carry on with this a bit later on? Maybe lunchtime - or how about I come over to your place this evening and we can look through the results together properly?"

"Yes, that makes more sense, and we'll have a lot more time to process it - we need to do this together, even if it's just me in the account at the moment."

It was a tough challenge for Andy not to dive straight in, but he kept curiosity in check. Heading across Bryant Park, Andy was thinking it would be a tough call to wait til tonight. Anyway, he had a half day conference this morning in the agency on AI in digital design, in a client meeting, so his mind would be kept busy.

He shared the news with Denny when he arrived at the office, "Not sure if I can wait to find out what connection it is. Gino's coming round this evening, so we can find out together."

"That's really cool, bud, how you two have really come together, it's amazing… like some primal instinctive force has drawn you together almost."

"That's a bit like what some of the subreddits and online forums have talked about. I can't get my head around how our relationship's developed. I suppose I'm not really analysing it - just going with it… and not having any of my usual misgivings and holding back. I'd usually be waiting to see what's on the other person's agenda. But it's not even crossed my mind here… that is so weird - but I guess we've both come at it from the same viewpoint - or a mirror imaged viewpoint, so it's also pretty wonderful."

"It's been great to watch. Hey, and Max and Michelle are fun people - how about the way he kept you secret from her. That's some stunt! And it was really cool seeing her reaction - exactly like my own two weeks ago! It was good to meet her… and they're not a couple? They sure look it."

"I think there was some history there, way back but they were colleagues before. Gino's been on a couple of dates with her but says she's more like one of the guys and didn't click. Not sure if she has a significant other. Mate. I'm sure we'll all meet up again sometime soon, if you want to check it out." Andy grinned.

He was looking forward to this evening and exploring the Ancestry results together with Gino. Working on something with his actual twin brother - for the first time in their lives. But for the moment, he had to immerse himself in the packaging brief and designing the pack structure for a baked goods range.

The evening came around soon enough, Gino arrived bringing pizza and salad, and they both settled at the breakfast bar, laptop open and ready. Andy picked out a couple of beers from the refrigerator, "Right, are you ready for this bro?"

Gino nodded - and Andy clicked on the Matches tab. And bingo, there appeared to be quite a few matches at 9% and 14% - and two others with a 25% match with one, Sinead as a potential Half Sister or Niece and the other, Niall as potentially a Half Brother or Nephew.

"Now that looks like a result! We have some relations! I guess we should follow up on these two first Andy. Can we see a family tree for either of them?"

The graphic came up and showed the O'Connor / Mc Dermott family group with both of them on there. They could see the previous generations though, and there was a branch of Kellys with Patrick and Margaret showing up as Sinead's grandparents.

Looking at some of the connections, it seemed that they were mostly from Waterford - Patrick showed as being born in County Waterford. There appeared to be way more boxes in the family tree than DNA matches, but they guessed that only a few of them will have got involved. They guessed that the ones showing as names had died - others showed as 'Living' including Niall and Sinead's mother and father.

"I wonder what they were looking for - maybe they are aware of us and searching. Might be that they can only see us if they still have a live Ancestry account; I read somewhere on here that even if they have dormant accounts, their details still show in the website. I'm not sure but even so, they could still be getting a notification themselves of a new match - same as we're seeing now. That could put the cat amongst the pigeons!"

"The what?" asked Gino, "British English is so quaint sometimes!"

"Hey, at least we can spell correctly!" grinned Andy. They'd had some of this banter in Dillon's the other night, with Andy's friendly jibe about Americans relying on a dictionary written by a dyslexic.

They both tried to read through the scant detail about the family "I say we just go in with both feet and contact these closest matches." Gino suggested.

The two most likely matches, at 25%, were Niall O'Connor and Sinead Mc Dermott. Gino was thinking about this, "Of course, there's no way of knowing if these matches are maternal or paternal is there?"

"Of course, we don't and that makes sense."

Andy started off drafting a new message, explaining the situation as diplomatically as he could, about having taken a test to find his birth mother. They edited and re-edited the message between them, and re-read it together:

Dear Sinead,

I hope that this may not come as too much of a shock to you, but it appears that we may well be connected, with about a 25% match in the Ancestry DNA website. From what I've read, that could mean that we are potentially cousins or half siblings. I have found a few other more distant matches in Ancestry, who could be cousins maybe.

As far as I know from our records, I was born in Dublin, to a woman called Brenda Kelly on 3rd August 1981. I was originally given the name Patrick.

I was then adopted from a Catholic charity by a couple in London, England. Out of thanks to the woman who gave birth to me, they kept Patrick as my middle name. I currently live and work as a graphic and digital designer in New York. If there is a connection, one of my main motivations was to let my birth mother know that I had a great and very happy adoption. My adopted parents are also supportive of me trying to find my birth mother.

It may not turn out to be the best policy, but they'd decided that it was too early to mention Gino as well just yet. Maybe a step too far.

Andy paused, "I think that's the right tone for this. Sound OK to you?"

"Yeah, not being too assumptive - or forceful, sounds good."

"This is going to be tough, we're about to just crash in, and maybe wreck what their family thought they knew about themselves. Especially so, if they knew nothing about us."

He teed the message up for the two closest contacts in the app and hit SEND. "Here goes - boom!"

Now it was just a matter of waiting.

— **12** —

Saturday, Sinead's reply

Just two days later Andy had taken a walk round to the Food Express for some weekend shopping, taking in the sights and morning buzz of Little Manila. Feeling his phone buzz, he saw he had had a response from one of the matches - Sinead Mc Dermott. He messaged Gino to let him know once he was back from the shop, suggesting a Zoom call again so they can both read it fresh.

Sinead's reply was quite a short message and they read together:

Dear Andrew,

I was fascinated to get your message, as I had not heard mention of you within the family.

You'd said you knew that your birth mother's name was Brenda Kelly. My own mother is Brenda O'Connor, and Kelly was her maiden name.

I spoke to my Mam to tell her that you had been in contact about a family connection, but she didn't seem to know anything really, just said 'Oh interesting, I wonder if we're related?'

I see that the Ancestry result shows us as being a 25% connection, so I'll have to explore that here among the family.

Kind regards

"So, it sounds as though she doesn't know if her mother was the same Brenda Kelly as ours. Like you said there could be loads with the same name in Dublin. But she was a 25% connection, so surely she has to be a half sister, no?"

"I wish it was clearer and more simple - I'd been thinking that as Kelly is one of the most common names in Ireland, it could be just as you say - that there are probably a few Brenda Kellys. It may not be her mother and maybe we are connected via her father. I guess we just have to wait…"

"…til the 'cat among the pigeons' calms down maybe," Gino grinned, "though we've not heard from Niall yet. He may come back with something."

They took a look at the other connections, trying to make sense of which possible 'cousin' they were related to, and tying them in with the family tree.

Andy told Gino that his Mum had said she was very keen to come and see them both soon. She'd planned to come across in a few months anyway, but this was too exciting for her to put it off. "Depending on the flights, she and Leon will be coming over towards the end of next week."

"I'll let Mom know, I'm sure she would love them to stay with her, if they'd like that."

"They've been looking at hotels near my place, like last time - but yes, I'll ask her. I'm sure the two Mums will have a *lot* to talk about, comparing notes about our childhood years. Let me know if your mum is OK with that idea."

"I'll not need to ask, Andy, she would absolutely revel in having people around her."

"That sounds lovely, Mum will love that, and they can get to know each other better." Andy thought, "Not sure how you're fixed this evening, but I'm heading to the Forest Hills bar to watch the Chelsea match later on if you're free Gino,"

"I'm not, I'm afraid - I decided to give dating another try. Meeting a girl called Crissy in Little Italy - a bit touristy but at least she chose Italian, so that's a good start."

"I can't wait to hear all about it - or as much as you'll share," Andy laughed.

Calling his mum later that afternoon, he told her about Gino's offer for them to stay with Angie.

"Are you sure she'd be OK with that Andrew?

"Mum, Gino is sure she would absolutely love to have you both. She would welcome the company, and she's got a big enough house - and I'm sure you two would find an awful lot to talk about, comparing me and Gino growing up."

"That will be wonderful then, love. Leon's found some reasonably priced flights leaving on Thursday, leaving around lunchtime and getting into the Kennedy Airport just after 4. I'll get him to send you all the details."

"That sounds great - I'll see if we can both be there to meet you. I was thinking I'll hire a larger car this time to make it easier to get about. The car club ones are mostly smaller sedans."

Andy messaged Gino later on from the Forest Hills bar, before the match started, with the flight details to see if he would like to - or could meet his Mum at JFK on Thursday. He didn't expect to hear back as he hoped Gino was too busy to be thinking about that this evening!

Mum's thoughts

"Oh my dear, I can't wait to see my boy again - and to meet his twin 'brother'. That felt a very odd thing to say about a... a stranger really; Leon is his brother. This is going to be a very interesting journey for them both and for Gino's mother.

"It will be lovely to meet her. I already feel a bond, with us both bringing up the boys who really should have been together all along. How wonderful that a chance meeting made that happen. It sounds like they've

already bonded themselves, how strange and amazing must that be for them?

"Joseph was less interested, which I thought odd, though Leon was his favourite. He'd never have said as much, I know. I'll make sure I keep him up on what's happening, as I'm sure Andrew will forget about letting him know.

"I can't believe I'll get to see them both together in only a few days. How very exciting!"

13

Wednesday - more from Sinead

Andy was busy tackling another food packaging design job, when he saw another notification pop up on his phone beside the keyboard. He'd taken to keeping it close by recently, with big ramp up in the number messages and notifications he'd been getting recently.

This time another Ancestry notification. Opening the app, he saw it was another message from Sinead. He called Gino to see how he was fixed later on, to look at it together.

"I can't come over during the day Andy, I'm across in Williamsburg today. Can you come over to Astoria after work? I can make some food."

"Sure - I'll pick up my laptop and some Chianti, if you're cooking Italian" he smiled.

"Perfect, Chianti's good - see you around 7 if that's OK "

Later that afternoon, Andy saw another ping from the app - this time, it was a message from Niall O'Connor. He messaged Gino, to let him know they'd have two to look at later. This could be interesting - resisting the temptation to look further, as he packed up his desk and powered down the Mac.

He thought again of how busy his phone was now, from only getting the occasional message at the start of this journey, to several a day, from his twin and potential siblings, was more than just a bit of a change. It was hard work finding a family, he smiled to himself.

Heading back across Bryant Park in the evening light to the subway, he pondered what might have happened, if he'd taken the job in the West End agency, on Great Portland Street. Certainly, Max wouldn't have seen him - their paths would just never have crossed. He may never even have thought about looking for a twin, let alone his birth mother.

He stopped off at the Sicilian food stand, to pick up some Cannoli on the way, to add to the wine as his contribution toward this evening - and headed for the subway steps. The clattering of the stainless steel sided subway cars coming in the station always seemed more agitated and violent, compared to the smooth humming deceleration of the old red tube trains his Dad used to drive. It made him think of times he and Leon would watch out to check which tube driver it was, as it came into the station, and wave to him - it was often one of Dad's friends.

This time, however, he was taking the W train to Astoria, and he took an UBER for the last part of the journey. He would usually have walked, but it had been a long day.

The cab pulled up outside Gino's place in Astoria. The door opened as he came up the steps, "Hey bro, how ya doing? I saw your cab arriving outside the window."

"I like the sound of that, I suppose that makes sense, calling ourselves something like that, brother - bro. It feels kind of right. Here you go, some Cannoli for later."

"Hey - sweet!"

"Ha ha - very." Andy countered, as they laughed.

Gino already had a Salsiccia sauce on the stove top cooking away, so as he put the pasta on to cook, Andy got his laptop out and opened the Ancestry app. They poured a glass of Chianti each, and sat down to open up the first of today's messages.

Hi Andrew,

I hope you're keeping well - I have a question to ask of you.

Talking with Mammy again today, I saw that she was

actually very upset, and once we started talking, she opened

up to me on the question of your connection with me and

Niall, and she told me some of her past I'd never heard before. She's never said a word in her life to anyone before about this.

She told me that she had been pregnant, before she and Daddy married, and that she had given birth to twin boys when she first came to Dublin. She didn't say much else, but that she'd kept it all to herself out of shame. So, looking at our DNA connection, the only thing I can think, is that perhaps you might have a twin brother out there somewhere - and if that's right, then we are half siblings from the look of it.

She is not in a good way in herself at the moment, having had to deal with all this coming out and thinking about what happened, all these years on. I told her what you'd said, and I think that beneath it all she is thrilled I think, to know you've had a good adoption. Would you by any chance have a photo of yourself you could share? I'm sure she would love that - and I would love to see it myself.

Kindest regards,

Sinead.

"Oh man! You were totally right bro - that cat of yours is well and truly among those Irish pigeons. So, she kept all that to herself all these years?"

"Yeah, that's huge - I can't imagine… I suppose that in Ireland, even in the 70s and 80s, being pregnant 'out of wedlock' was a huge taboo. I think I've read that contraception was only legalised there sometime around then - and knowing the strength of the Catholic Church, it was probably only for actual 'family planning' purposes."

"Wow, that's even later than New York! I'd love to know more but it does sound like Brenda might be finding this very difficult - telling her daughter about us.

"You're right, especially as she'd not told anyone before - that's a whole new can of worms."

"True, I guess we should break off and eat now - and 'digest' all that from Sinead. This is seriously heavy - and we should come back to the message from Niall afterwards. Make sense?"

"Absolutely bro, that cooking smells pretty good - I should have brought a couple of bottles over."

"No problem, there's plenty more in the closet - how about a Cirò, a Calabrian wine from my Nonna's home town. It's great that I can find it now in a few wine shops downtown. Hopefully it will mask my cooking!"

Gino shared out the pasta and sauce, and they sat down to eat. Andy tasting his first glass of Cirò. "This is a very special wine Gino - and I'll also say that there's nothing wrong with your cooking. That is a really good sauce."

"I've had a good teacher, and years of practice cooking for myself - that's why I've made double - some for the freezer for next week to keep organized. That's the result of not finding the right girl I guess."

"Yeah, you have to learn how to cook - and all the rest. Hey, I meant to ask, how did it go with Crissy at the weekend?"

"Well… she was fun, good sense of humour, and she's stylish and looks after herself… and you know…" he smiled, "I don't know what else I'm looking for - perhaps that should be enough?"

"I know what you mean. And my mum keeps telling me that I need to find someone who will be a best friend as well. You said you'd been out with Michelle a few times, she seems like a good friend, and a really nice woman - still single as well?"

"Yeah, I know all that, but we've known each other for years and years, so she's like one of the boys. It just never worked, at least for me. Almost feels wrong somehow. I might try seeing Crissy again - see how keen she is."

"It may not all be lost with Michelle, based on the way she was looking at you in the bar last week. There's something there, I'm sure."

"Hey - she was looking at the both of us. It was the weirdness of the situation - she was checking us both out. It's not often you run across identical twins, especially a *new* identical twin of someone you know - that in itself must be truly weird," Gino laughed.

They finished up and took another glass and a Cannoli each back to the laptop to tackle the second message of the day - from Niall.

Dear Andrew,

Thanks for your message in this app. That was certainly a shock - even more so now that I've spoken to Sinead. She told me that she'd written to you about our Mam's state of mind, and how she'd said she had twins in 1981. Do you know anything about the other baby at all? It for sure sounds as if we are related and I'm wondering if the other child survived. On the genetics of it, a 25% match seems pretty strong, so it does seem likely we might well be half brothers.

Sinead and I only joined up on this website to see if we could find Dad's cousins who ended up in Australia. No luck on that though so far.

I'm not sure if Sinead updated you on our family at this end. She'd told you that Mammy's maiden name was Kelly of course, as I'm sure you've seen in the family tree on there. She married our Daddy in Dublin - he had been her childhood sweetheart down in Waterford. Mammy told us that they found each other again here in Dublin, and were

married soon after that.

Sinead's the big sister, then comes myself - and we have

three younger sisters: Aisling, Niamh and Maireadh.

It sounds like Sinead's totally on the case here, and we all

talk often in the family, so I'm thinking it's easier if you

carry on messaging with her rather than duplicating it all to

me as well - and we'll all talk at this end.

Anyhow, this sounds like it's all very exciting - and I'm

looking forward to finding out more about yourself.

Best regards

Niall O'Connor

"Sensible chap that," Andy was thinking, "I think that it's now time to go back to Sinead, and give her the news that the other twin has been found. I'm sure she'd find the story fascinating."

"That makes sense - why not - let's blow her mind again! OK, let's put a message together now, and drop the next bit of news on them. I wonder if it's possible to Cc Niall in the app?"

"I don't think so from the look of this... but he said to send messages to Sinead anyway. OK, let's have a go at this." They drafted and tweaked a couple of times and finished with:

Hi Sinead,

Many thanks for your message and I'm sorry if I've caused

unhappy memories to be brought up. I was acutely aware

that could be the case and tried to be as diplomatic as I could

- but I'm a graphic designer and not a wordsmith!

Yes I'd be happy to share a photo - but first I've a little more news that both you and Niall raised, about my twin. That's actually the strangest part of it from my end. I actually met him only very recently; in fact, a couple of weeks ago and entirely by chance - and it was the strangest chance. We had not known anything at all about each other until then.

As I mentioned I was brought up in London, and had a good adoption with a lovely couple. I moved to New York two years ago for work, and quite by chance somebody spotted me in the city and completely mistook me for my twin. I followed up on that, and then met Gino Bianchi, who had been adopted by an Italian American couple over here. We found out that we share the same birth date, and as we actually look so alike, we carried out a familial DNA test, which was pretty conclusive that we are genetically identical twins.

I'll send the photo after this in a second message, so that it's not too much of a shock for you both. Gino and I decided that just one of us should start the Ancestry search, so as not to confuse things. We would both love a picture or two of you all as well and see if we look like anyone.

I do hope that your mother isn't finding all this news too distressing. We are both intensely grateful to her for giving us the gift of life, and hope we can meet at some point, if that's what she wishes.

"Nicely put man. I thought you said you're not a 'wordsmith'; those words look pretty well 'smithed' to me. And yeah, that was always something for me growing up. I never looked like anyone in my family. And boy, has that changed! It would be nice to see if we look anything like the rest of the family."

It was getting late now and the bottle of Cirò was nearly done. Andy said, "I've got an early start in the morning, with a conference call briefing with a client in Europe, so I'd better get off soon."

"So, your Mom's arriving tomorrow - what time does she get in? Mom cannot wait to meet her."

"They're due at 16:10 into Terminal 8."

"I'll leave the office early and go straight out to mom's and be there to meet you all."

"I've hired a bigger sized car for the time they're here, and added Leon as a driver, so they can all get about. I'm sure they'll find that useful while staying with your mother, and I'm sure she'll want to show my Mum the sights."

"Great that sounds perfect - Mom's not the most confident driver these days. We should all have some good times meeting up and you're right, she'll want to show your 'mum' around."

Mam's thoughts

"Who'd have thought that after all these years? Oh, those two beautiful boys - that broke my heart giving them up despite how that all happened. I knew in my heart, it would be the best thing for their own sakes, the poor mites - not that I had any choice over the matter. And what did I have to offer them?

"Then my Michael came and found me in Dublin, and we kept all that to ourselves ever since. I loved him so dearly for wanting to marry me,

72

even after I'd told him why I was sent away, and the babies - and the shame of the Magdalen and everything. He was - still is - my strength. Our Sinead's inherited some of his grit and determination, so she has.

"Once we had the children, I wasn't strong enough to tell anyone about it all; I couldn't drag them into being tarnished with the shame - especially my baby, dear Maireadh. It was all kept under the mat. But, maybes I can, now that so much is out there now, in these TV shows about the laundries - I remember watching that 'Ireland's Dirty Laundry' programme, and I just wept. Sinead wondered what it was upsetting me so - but of course I just said it's the sadness of it all. How could the church have allowed - or actually devised all that evil - and forced it on so many women.

"What a time - yes broke my heart they did - and those bastard nuns so nearly broke the rest of me. I'm just thankful that Sister Hilda saw something in my grasp of arithmetic, to suggest me for the bookkeeping job in the town, or I might have still been washing priests' cassocks like those other beggars into the '90s.

"It is important that I tell the whole story to Sinead - and Niall maybe as they're the oldest - and tell them about it all - the whole sorry story. Let's have this out in the open so they can understand what broke me - who I've been - and why I've done what I've done all through my life."

14

Thursday - two mothers meet

Thursday had started very early for Andy. It was amazing how much quieter the subway was even just an hour or so earlier than usual.

There was no-one else in the studio when he arrived for the conference call, which went smoothly enough. He would have to get the important stuff from the briefing properly underway, ready to hand over to the team if needed.

He was getting more done as well before everyone else turned up for work - 'well, there's no-one around to waste time chatting to,' he thought. So he was properly prepared, to hand things over to Denny, in time for his early finish.

The morning passed quickly, and he waved at Denny as he left in the early afternoon, for his time off to greet his Mum and Leon.

He made his way to the subway out to JFK to collect the Lincoln Navigator he'd hired from the rental office. He was thinking it made sense to have something big enough to pick them both up and the luggage up at the airport, and then possibly ferry everyone else around, a 7-seater made sense. As he stepped in to drive off he realised what a huge vehicle it was!

He parked up in the pick up zone for Terminal 8 and walked towards the arrivals hall to wait for them, getting a coffee as he was a few minutes early. He positioned himself at the exit door from Arrivals, to wait and catch a glimpse of them coming through the doors.

"Hi Leon, Mum," he waved, and shouted above the noise. Leon returned the wave, and steered the cases through the exit, and they all pulled together in a hug.

"So wonderful to see you Andrew, is it just you meeting us?"

"Yes. Gino's at his mom's already - I've got a car hired to run you up to Angie's place on the Island - and like I said, Leon, you're a named driver on it. I can't park a car easily at my place - and certainly not this monster, so you can use it for trips out while you're here. It should take us about an hour getting there, once we're out of the airport traffic."

The drive to Glen Cove took them North on the Cross Island, then joining the Grand Central Parkway. As they turned off along the Glen Cove Road, Jeannette was taking in the scenery as they drove through the trees, and caught glimpses of the larger houses set back from the road, "There's some lovely looking houses around here - these are all a lot bigger than my place in Morden," she said, smiling.

"Yep - everything's oversized here." As he took the left turn on the way into Glen Cove, Andy was thankful for the GPS, satnav guiding him through the maze of streets in Sea Cliff, to Angie's house. He turned off the road and pulled onto the driveway in front of her neat house, where she and Gino were stood on the porch waiting to greet them.

"Oh Jeannette, you look as lovely as Andy says you are!" Jennette gave Andy 'the look' as Angie gave her a hug and laughed.

"Angie it is so lovely to meet you - and oh my gosh - you too dear Gino. I feel I know you already, Andrew has told me so much about you."

"Welcome to New York Jeannette - can I call you that?"

"Of course, this is no time to be formal, it almost feels like you're family already anyway," as she gave him a brief hug.

Angie ushered them in and through to the kitchen, "Now who would like a coffee? Gino, Andy? Or would you prefer tea Jeannette, how do you take it?"

"Tea would be lovely. Splash of milk and no sugar thanks, and probably the same for Leon."

Gino led them out to the seating on the terrace - where they could take in the view, out over the trees and all Angie's hard work, making the back yard look at its best for early summer. A sweeping lawn led the eye down the slight grade. Angie loved the sweep of Rhododendrons and Azaleas leading down around the path to the trees at the far end. She also cherished her stands of roses starting to flower nearer the terrace, originally planted by Joe.

"What a beautiful garden Angie,' Jeannette smiled, "I just love those Azaleas - such colours - we really have chosen the best time to come and visit you."

"Why thank you so much. Yes I adore them, even if we only get the treat of the blooms for a short while. And even the roses are flowering already. Well, it's been a little warmer this spring, which helps." she laughed. "Now, I don't know how hungry you both are. Airline food leaves me cold, and I guess you'll have been given some kind of random snack before landing."

"I had a bit of the 'lunch' they called it, but Mum couldn't be bothered with it." Leon said.

"Well in that case you'll need something simple and decent inside you."

"It just so happens that Mom has rustled up 'something simple' - she's actually been cooking all day," laughed Gino.

"Oh, hush you Gino! I have a nice tomato and basil Caprese for you, to start, and then we can have some Lasagna and salad; I hope that sounds OK, Jeannette."

"Ooh yes, wonderful."

They moved to the kitchen and Jennette offered to help with anything - as mothers do. Andy and Gino watched them and smiled at each other, "It's like they're the twins, these two."

"Ha ha - too right Andy! Hey Leon, fancy a beer or a glass of wine to go with dinner?"

"A beer would be great Gino, thanks. Should I bring our luggage in from the car first, while they're busy in the kitchen? Save doing it all later on." They unloaded the trunk, and Gino went up to show him their bedrooms. "Your Mom has an ensuite, and the family bathroom is this one on the left for you."

"Thanks so much for this Gino - it really is much appreciated."

"So much better than some soulless Manhattan or Queens hotel we thought. It will give our mothers more time together to talk about us and share stories." The three 'boys' headed back down to the kitchen and Gino took some beers and wine out to the terrace, where everything was ready to eat.

The Caprese looked fresh and delicious. "I'm afraid I didn't grow these tomatoes - too early here - but the rucola and lollo rosso salad is some of the early crop from my own garden, round the side of the house there." she said.

"So not only cooked with love - grown with love," added Gino.

The lasagna was so good, Andy looked up from his plate, "Angie this is quite a different lasagna, I love the sausage through it."

"Another of my Nonna's recipes, so I take little credit for it - keeping a bit of Calabria bubbling away out here on Long Island."

"Oh no, you take the credit; it takes skill - and love as Gino said - to make food this good. And your boy here proved to me that he's not a bad cook himself, you certainly passed on the best of Calabria there."

"You know, Jeannette. I think between us, we've not done a bad job of bringing these two boys up. Your Andy is such an English gentleman - and you know, I am proud of how Gino turned out - how they both turned out I guess." she laughed - then looking more thoughtful, "And what did you think of the message the boys had back from the Irish family? At least they now know there are two of you boys."

"I know, that was the trickiest part. Keeping it as just Andy contacting them made sense at first, as they came back asking about 'the other baby', which made it easier to bring me into the picture."

"It was - as you've said before Andrew - it's like we're watching our very own 'Long Lost Family' - which I know we both love watching Angie - and finding out the next stage in real time. It is so exciting. I'm thinking you must feel a bit left out of it all Leon." as she smiled at him.

"Not in the least Mum. It's just as fascinating for me. I've always known Andy was 'chosen', as you put it, which made it feel special for him. It's great that he - and Gino - can let the woman that gave birth to them, know just how they turned out. I'm sure she'll not be too disappointed," they laughed.

"What a lovely thought that is Jeannette, Andy being 'chosen' - I wish I'd thought of that - but I'm going to use it from now on!" Angie stood up, "right, coffees and Sfogliatella next. Let's go and sit down in the lounge - we've got so much to talk about."

Andy and Gino shared a cab back to Queens later on. "Another momentous day - it seems to be each day brings something massive to deal with - or to enjoy."

Gino laughed, "I know what you mean. I was comparing the past few weeks to the same time last year - or even last month. I've never had so much going on before. It sure changes your world view, being a twin brother. That in itself takes some getting my head around."

"It does indeed." Andy and Gino talked through how they both ended up in creative work, with Angie wondering where they got it from. "You know your mom doesn't realise it but she is very creative in her own way. Having the vision to create that lovely garden - with having to plan years ahead for how it will look later. That's some skill."

"The backyard you mean," laughed Gino.

"Ah yep, what was it Churchill had said; 'two great nations separated by the same language' or something like that." They laughed. The cab worked its way back west towards Queens and home for them both.

Mom's thoughts

"Jeannette really is lovely - almost like an English version of me. I guess we end up shaped by our children a bit, so maybe that's not a surprise. And Leon is another credit to her, such a gentleman. I must say, I never liked those 'dreads' too much, but he carries it off well.

"Hearing about her Joseph was interesting; how he moved to England from Barbados. That would have been a culture shock for them, and I

didn't know there was such a racial situation like she described. Nowhere near the way we had over here of course - or still have in the South from what I see in the news.

"And it all got me wondering how that poor Brenda is coping with it all coming out. It sounds like it's been a guilty secret for over 40 years. How could she have carried on with her not knowing anything about them - I hope she is getting some comfort from knowing her babies are both well - and back together."

15

Friday - more about Mam

Late Friday afternoon as Andy was finishing off the week's work and scheduling for Monday, he had another notification in Ancestry. Checking the phone app, he saw it was from Sinead again. He called Gino to see how he was fixed to meet or Zoom and read it together.

"Hey, I'm just closing up the office shortly, so now works for me. Give me 5 minutes."

Andy sorted out his password so he could login on to Ancestry on his work Mac and had it fired up ready and send the Zoom link to Gino. "So I've just had this one, so no idea what she's coming back with. I hope her Mum's OK," as he clicked 'share screen'.

"Yeah - let's take a look…" the message opened…

Hi Andy - and Gino,

Me and Niall have been talking more with Mam since your message, along with our sisters. Your news really was quite something and took all our breaths away. It was so wonderful to hear about you both. What a story that is - and thank you so so much for that photo. I can see something of us all in your faces - I hope you can too in the photo I just sent over.

Mam has been really deeply affected, as having to deal with all of this after so many years has taken it out of her; I came over and stayed with her last night. But I think it has been the best thing that could have happened for her in a lot of ways.

Not only has she been able to share some of her life in Waterford that we'd not known about, she talked us through what was such an awful and harrowing story of your birth. No pain relief and no real care.

We thought about the idea of doing a Zoom call as there's another part to Mam's story that really won't bear being shared in a mere message, if that would work for you both. Perhaps we can do that over the weekend and I can let you know more. I've added my email and mobile number for WhatsApp below to arrange it.

I can't wait to actually talk to and see you both.

Best

Sinead and family

"Wow, that's…" Andy looked at Gino. "This really did drop like a bombshell for their whole family. I'll go back to her and say yes, if that works for you and suggest tomorrow morning at 9, before we go up to your mom's house? That'll be their afternoon."

"Sure, that sounds ideal. I'll come over to your place first."

Andy wrote a quick reply to Sinead to say that a Zoom call with them sounded a great idea - and how about tomorrow - 2pm Dublin time - and copied the same message to her email address with a Zoom invite attached. She replied pretty much straight away and accepted.

"So that's settled bro. I can't think what is worse, that she doesn't want to share in a message"

"Too right - I guess we'll have to wait, and be prepared. See you tomorrow bro - I'll bring some fresh bread."

They signed off, both left wondering what it could be - what was coming next.

16

Saturday Zoom with Sinead

Gino's cab pulled up outside Andy's place in Woodside early on the Saturday morning, and buzzed his apartment. "Hi, I've brought a baguette and croissants for breakfast bro!"

"Come right up Gino… and there's coffee here too if you want it. Bang on time…" Andy had finished setting the laptop up ready for their call with Sinead, "ah here she is…"

A second face appeared in the Zoom window as Gino sat down. "Well good morning, Sinead."

"Well good afternoon to you two. I really can't believe any of this is actually happening," she almost giggled, "but so much is falling into place now, more than ever now, seeing your faces… and oh my, how alike you are. More so than even the photo you sent. Oh, and I can see so much of my Mammy in you." She was right, even from the small family snap she'd sent over, it was clear where they'd got their eyes from. "So, which of you is which?"

"I'm Gino, the one with a neater haircut." nudging Andy with a smile, "and yes, I can see something of me even in your face, and definitely your hair colour."

"We are so happy you thought about this call," added Andy, "there is so much we want to ask about your mum and our birth - and you suggested there was something else we needed to know?"

Sinead hesitated, as she looked a little more serious, "yes, indeed there is… I told you that Mammy said that she'd had twin babies when she was very young, just 17 - so that would have been in 1981, and your birth date is what she remembers. When I told her

3rd of August was your birthday, she broke down, remembering being pregnant in the July heat and then…"

Niall appeared with two mugs of tea at their end, "Sorry for being late. Important job this one," as he gestured 'cheers', "Yes, sorry to butt in. Yes, she'd never spoken about it to any of us before about all this; we had no idea at all, so this has come as… as a real shock, so it has."

"Indeed it was," Sinead continued, "though the giving birth was almost the least of her troubles. She had a God-awful time of it that I'd… none of us ever had any clues about. All we knew was that she'd come up to Dublin from County Waterford, for a job at the stationery company. But that was such an… almost… or yes, it was a cover up for her real story, so it was. In fact, like an awful lot of other young girls who had babies out of wedlock, they were forced to… pay for their sins, like an atonement. Their penance being to have to work in the nuns' laundries. Magdalenes, they were called."

Sinead was appearing more emotional, "This has been such a painful thing for her to re-live. The TV and papers have been bringing out a lot more information recently about these Magdalene laundries, and the experiences that our mam and thousands of other women went through here in Ireland - you may not have heard of it. But I think she almost felt emboldened by knowing that others like Elizabeth Coppin have been fighting back against all the injustice. And as our Daddy is not too well - we think it's early Alzheimer's - maybe she felt that all this coming out now maybe wouldn't harm him or his memories of back then."

Niall went on, "You see, she'd fallen in the family way when only 16, living in a village near Waterford. Mam told us what happened; a family friend had cornered her, and forced himself on her. Granda wouldn't believe her, but it soon became clear something had happened. So, the parish priest had told them that he'd arranged for her to stay in a mother and baby home in a Dublin Convent, where she'd be cared for by the nuns until the birth. And then she'd be given 'a job in Dublin'."

Sinead's face betrayed a deep anger, "...being 'cared for' was not at all what she got."

Sensing that they may not be too aware of any of this, he added, "I suppose I need to add a bit of context. You see back then, Ireland was just a bit backward, and especially for the 'Culchies' down there in the bog country. It would have been a huge scandal to be expecting a baby, and even if she'd stayed, she'd have never found a husband down there. So 'having a job arranged for her' was the usual way for families to deal with it, like Sinead said."

"So, she gave birth to two babies, pretty obviously yous two," Sinead smiled, "and then had to nurse you for about 6 weeks until you were ready to be adopted. So as she said, she'd had time to get to know the two of you and to grow to love you."

Sinead was tearful on screen, "And here's where it gets almost more awful. As soon as you'd both been taken away from her, she was transferred to the Magdalene Laundry in Sean MacDermott Street in Dublin as a 'penance' for her sins. So that was the 'job in Dublin'," she almost spat it out, "- and there were these laundries run by nuns all over Ireland - horrendous, so it was. The bloody Catholic Church of all things! The girls weren't paid anything - just bed and board in what amounted to a prison - they couldn't even get out! It gets me so angry, now that I know more about it all."

Andy and Gino were both shaken, "So, she ended up working in the laundry straight after giving birth?"

"No, no, not so cushty as all that. The new girls had to do their *penance* for being fallen women. She was put to scrubbing floors for three months, before going on to sorting the priests' dirty laundry. It makes my blood boil, so it does."

"I suppose you may have picked up that our Sinead is none too impressed with our dear mother church, eh?" Niall smiled sardonically.

"I think I'm beginning to - and starting to feel the same," agreed Andy, "and I've only just heard all this. So, I remember watching a BBC documentary a while back about the Magdalene laundry in Cork. Are you saying they were all over the place?"

"Ah yes, so they were - in almost every town. It was like a modern day slavery, and thank God, were finally all closed down back in the 90s - the Dublin one Mam was at, I found out, was closed in '96. The government has officially apologised to the Irish people for being complicit in the practice - years too late - and there's all manner of court cases going on, and the government 'restitution' has only started to pay compensation to victims over more recent years. It's a humungous mess, so it is."

Niall comforted his sister, "The top and bottom of this, lads is that at last, my Mam feels as though she can let go of all that bottled up anger, at what she was put through by priests and nuns, and the whole fixed system. I don't know how she lived with it, keeping that all hidden and eating away at her. I hope she can get to do what others have done and seek some redress and compensation for it all."

"Sounds like it's all too little too late. Always the way if it's the authorities being held to account," offered Gino. "So how did she escape from the laundry? It sounds like women were stuck there for years."

"I suppose it must have been a stroke of luck - or two really, Gino." he nodded, "Ah, Jaysus, I can still barely tell yous two apart! Well, Mam was always good with arithmetic at school back in Waterford. So the nuns had given her a kind of book-keeping role, dealing with the records of the laundry coming in and out. The second stroke of luck was one of the nuns actually had a heart, from the sound of it. She picked her out for a real job on the outside, bookkeeping clerk, for a stationery company in Dublin."

"That was the bit we did know about," Sinead added.

"It wasn't all good," Niall continued, "as from what Mam said, she had to leave the Magdalene straight after breakfast for her first day at work, with just the clothes she could pick out from the unclaimed items. And as there was no state assistance available to them, she went to the new job on a Monday morning straight from the laundry, with just the clothes she stood up in - no money - nowhere to live. If it hadn't been for the kindness of one of her new colleagues who let her use their spare room until she got on her feet, Lord only knows what would have become of her."

They moved on to lighter things about the family, with Sinead giving a quick description of the other three sisters, "Aisling is similar to me, a bit er…"

"A bit gutsy, she's trying to say."

"Oh, shush you, Niall - but I suppose it is. Niamh is a bit studious and then Maireadh is artistic and sensitive - like me," she said pointedly, looking at Niall - both of them smiling. "So, we're quite a close family I think it's fair to say. Would you agree?"

"Yes, Sinead's bang on there, we're pretty close knit, so we are - but hell, I've no idea how Mammy kept all of this to herself all these years, so I don't."

They ended the call, "We should all speak again soon, or have another call or something, lads."

"Absolutely Niall, and we'd love to be able to talk to Brenda at some point, but only when she is ready of course."

"Well, we'll speak to yous both soon then and message in between," Sinead waved as she ended the call.

— 17 —

Saturday with 2 Mums

After their conversation with Sinead and Niall, the twins were both a bit subdued, barely speaking as they rode the LIRR from Jamaica to Glen Cove. Deep in thought, looking out of the train windows but not really registering anything, after their harrowing call with their Irish siblings. There were no words that could deal with what they'd just been told.

Andy was pondering how they would relay the news they had just had from Sinead and Niall. "This is going to be a tough morning - not least for two ladies who were brought up believing in a loving Catholic church. I'm not sure how I can deal with what I just heard myself. This 'loving church' imposed on these poor victims, what I can only think of as an institutional evil."

Gino just nodded. As the train pulled into the Sea Cliff station, they saw Leon in the enormous black SUV waiting for them in the car park and waved.

"So, you got used to driving this wardrobe of a car then, Leon?"

"It's more like a luxury garden shed, Andy. You'd never get this parked anywhere in London, it's monstrous. And I definitely need the reversing camera to work out how long it is even!"

"You did pick the biggest thing around Andy," laughed Gino.

"I was thinking that there may be trips out that we might all want to take, and this seats seven. Plus, I knew Leon would appreciate how eco-friendly it was - NOT," he smirked.

"I get it bro, the perfect team bus."

They'd arrived in time for coffee on the terrace. Another bright day which helped to lift the twins' mood a little, as they fell into conversation about yesterday's trip, out along to the Hamptons, and the two mothers' discussions from last evening.

"Did you have a good day yesterday, Angie - you two got a lot of talking done?"

"We certainly did, Andy. We took your mother on a trip out east to the Hamptons, had a nice lunch and then took in LongHouse gardens, which are so beautiful at this time of year. I'd not been there since I last went with Joe, so it was nice to visit with these two."

"Oh yes, such lovely gardens - more of those gorgeous Azaleas. A perfect time of year to visit, oh and those sculptures Angie, a really unique kind of place. It was wonderful! We had such a lovely day; not sure it was all up Leon's street," he smiled back, "and all those huge posh houses that look like they're from Bing Crosby films."

"A lot of them are Jeannette - quite a few movies have been shot out here," Gino added.

"We even passed a Vineyard, which I wasn't expecting; a really nice drive out there, Long Island seems to go on forever - the name makes sense I suppose. Yes, it was a lovely day out Mum, maybe something we should do more at home."

Andy and Gino turned the chat back to their mothers' conversations about their adoptions from earlier. Trying to gently ease into the difficult task of relating what Sinead and Niall had told them. "We spoke to Sinead and her brother Niall this morning, mum,"

"Oh Andy, that's wonderful news, isn't it Angie."

"It is. Andy had a message yesterday late afternoon, and they'd suggested having a call over Zoom - like we did in lockdown, Mom. They had told us that their mom had opened up about our birth. Us two reappearing after all these years has really dropped a bombshell on their family."

Andy took up the thread, "Sinead had said in her email, that there was a lot more of the story they'd not wanted to tell us in a simple message."

"Oh my, you dear boys," Angie squeezed Gino's arm, "I can't think what on earth could have been worse than what she'd already been through?"

Andy sighed, "Well there was more, a lot more. She went through so much." He and Gino then recounted all the details from their Zoom conversation, on the Magdalene laundries, the treatment, the awful sounding nuns and systematic cruelty, all orchestrated by the Church, and with the Irish state being complicit. They also shared how Sinead was almost incandescent with rage over the revelations.

Angie looked horrified. "You know, we were recommended to that adoption charity in Dublin, because Joe and I told the church that we did not want to be party to what was going on here in New York. The Church itself over here seemed to be running a scam - I can't recall all the details from way back when, they called it the 'baby scoop', I think, in the newspapers - and Joe was so angry about it all. That's why we flew over to Dublin to adopt you, son."

Jeannette was equally shocked, going over their account in her mind, "how could a society - and more shockingly, the Church... our Church, think that a set up like that was a Christian way of dealing with things? Dear God, my heart really goes out to Brenda, the poor dear... and to her children. Fancy having to find out all this about your own mother in such a way. It's little wonder that Sinead was so angry," looking across at Angie, "and our Church? How could that kind of thing happen?"

"Too easily Jeannette. We even had priests running baby farms over here. I think there has been a lot of soul searching - at long last - among the Church hierarchy... and hopefully making amends."

"The one real positive for us," Andy added, "was that we actually got to see people that looked a bit like Gino and me; Niall even had our dimple in his chin. We'd said a while back, that's a thing we'd not really had before - looking like someone."

Gino nodded, "Sinead and Niall both seem really nice people - and already so accepting of us. I guess this could have gone either way - they really could have resented us, being the cause of all this stuff coming out into the open; the thing their mom had kept secret, out of shame I guess, for her whole life."

"I'm feeling that maybe our appearance and… and the upset it caused, has been somehow… cathartic for them? It's sure as hell stirred things up, and brought a lot of emotion to the surface - Sinead certainly showed us that. I was wondering about us going over to meet them, Gino - maybe message her and suggest it."

"Oh my dear Gino, I never thought about that side of things; of you not looking like someone else in the family."

"And I reckon that will have been even more of a problem for you Andy, with me looking more like our Dad? And it didn't help that I hung out with my own crew at school."

"We had to find our own 'crews', I suppose Leon. And hey," Andy smiled, "I've found someone here who looks just a little bit like me now." They laughed at that. Jeannette and Angie moved to the kitchen to get some lunch prepared, while the three boys talked about their life in Queens.

Leon told them a bit more about yesterday's trip, "Mum loved it, and we've been planning where else to go. She said she'd love to go and see Coney Island Gino, what's it like?"

"It can be a lot of fun, some really old-school wooden roller coasters, fairground rides and a long boardwalk - and real proper Hot Dogs and just a lot of nostalgia. I guess a bit like your Blackpool, but brasher and grittier I'd guess. I'm sure your mom would love it."

"She's also got some of the places in Manhattan in her sights - Empire State, Central Park, Ground Zero, which she said she'd missed seeing last time she came over here. I can ferry her about to some of the places, but I suppose the train is probably quicker from here, eh?"

"Absolutely, Leon. You can go from where you picked us up earlier - the LI-double-R takes you straight into Manhattan into Penn Station and you can take subways all up and downtown. You'll be best getting a 7 day MetroCard when you get into town."

As they ate lunch, Gino asked Jeannette about the places she wanted to visit while she was in New York, "Leon said you want to see Coney Island?"

"Oh yes, it's one of those places - it's always talked about in the films. It's just a case of saying that I've been to see it, I suppose."

"How about we take a trip out after lunch? suggested Gino. "We could all go down in the car, and maybe get some dinner out later on? What do you think Mom?"

"Sure, why not - I've not been for years!" she laughed.

They all piled into the Lincoln after lunch, and Leon drove off towards Coney Island, joining the traffic on the roads skirting the outskirts of JFK airport, and on to find a parking lot near the boardwalk. As they took the path towards the beach, the sunshine on the water made them all feel that bit younger, and call to mind their family times at the beach - here for Gino - and at Southend for Andy. "Perfect seaside weather isn't it, just like it used to be. Though memory is always a bit rosier - we always blank out the days of rain, stuck in the caravan." Jeannette recalled.

The gentle breeze was lifting the row of flags above the food kiosks nearing the Luna Park funfair, with the halyards clanging against the flagpoles. "I guess after that lunch, we'll not need a visit to Nathan's this time - that's the famous Hot Dog stand here," Gino explained, "we'd always get one when Max and I came here as kids."

Jeannette remarked at how wide the boardwalk was. Angie told her, "On Sunday afternoons years ago, this would be full to both sides with folks out from the city to get some sea air." There were still quite a few families out walking, even this early in the season.

They stopped at a proper Italian Gelato ice-cream stand along the front and carried on walking, taking in the views and enjoying their ice-creams.

"So was this how you imagined Coney Island, Jeannette?

"Well, it's a lot more colourful than it looked in the old films," she laughed, "but yes I suppose it is really. It's like Southend that we used to go to when we were small - or Blackpool as Gino said, but on a much bigger scale."

"It's like I said, Mum. Same as everything over here," laughed Andy.

Gino had booked a table for them at an Italian place near Woodside, "it wasn't easy finding an Italian in 'Little Manila'," he joked. Over dinner, they talked through how they would tell their friends the details of the latest news, "- they'll need another episode of the 'Missing Twins Podcast' for all this," joked Gino. "But more seriously, we could do with it not being another Tuesday in the Irish bar."

"Perhaps we should do some food for them at my place?"

"Maybe - though I may have more space for them all at mine. Max needs space to expand! That's if we can get the team together," he laughed.

As they separated, Andy brought up the idea of hearing what Sinead would think about them meeting up - that they go to Dublin. "I'm wondering what Brenda - Mam would think about meeting us as well. It may be too soon for her? Best if we let Sinead decide I guess."

"Hell yeah, that would be amazing Andy, a massive step - and another podcast instalment! I've never been there either, so that will be a first."

"I'll send a WhatsApp and put the idea to them - something they'll need to all discuss together I'd reckon. It may take a while to decide - they might think it's too soon after this all hit the fan, and need time to let the dust settle, if that's not too many metaphors to mash together."

Mum's thoughts

"What a wonderful day, having both my boys together.

"It's truly amazing how quickly I feel close to Angie, such a lovely person and we had such a good time talking about these twin boys. And yes there are so many similarities between them, even some of the mannerisms. I've no idea how that works. I'm looking forward to them coming back tomorrow - and to finding out what Angie's 'Sunday Gravy' is all about of course.

"I so love the way they are together, it's like they've known each other for ever - not just these last few weeks. Maybe it's helped that they've got a common purpose, in discovering their birth mother. Now that's so

exciting - for dear Brenda, it does sound as though she can at last deal with all the awful stuff that happened when she was still so young - not much more than a child herself really.

"Andrew's idea to go and meet them all would be good, and Sinead sounds like a nice person from what the boys have said. And just thinking about how I would feel in her shoes, I'm sure Brenda would want to meet them at last."

—— 18 ——

Making 'Sunday Gravy'

Andy was awake early again on Sunday, with his mind buzzing on all that he - or rather, they had been learning. The morning looked bright and clear, so he set out for a gentle run around his local area in Woodside, thinking through the idea of meeting their birth family. Last night he'd sent a WhatsApp to their Irish family group chat, putting the idea out there, about him and Gino flying over to meet their new Irish family.

Niall had messaged back while he was out, and Andy pulled up at a crosswalk to read the message - yes Niall had replied, and agreed, 'that would be a grand idea, we'd love to see you'. As he was reading the message, he saw Gino had already answered, 'that's great - glad you like the idea', and then messaged Andy as well, 'Yep, we've some organizing to do bro!' - Andy added 'great - can't wait', and carried on with his run towards home, to get ready to go back out to Glen Cove; Angie was preparing to cook her famous Sunday Gravy again for her guests.

Jeannette had been helping Angie with some of the preparation during the morning. She was thinking, as they brought out big chunks of meat and sausage, as well as canned tomatoes, she was thinking that this was going to be very strange gravy. Nothing at all like the dark brown Bisto her mum used to serve up.

Angie put her right on it being the Sunday tradition of long cooked meat dishes, "some folks call theirs the 'Sunday Sauce' but it's the same; just real good ingredients, cooked together with a lot of love, for a long time."

Jeannette had loved working together with Angie, slicing onions and browning the pork shoulder and oxtail pieces, to assemble and set on the stove top, to come together ready for when the boys arrived later on.

Leaving it to cook away gently on the stove top, Angie took Jeannette on the short trip to where the Sunday walking group were meeting up this morning, a bit further up the hill to join the other ladies for a trip out to Garvies Point. As one of the ladies said, "it's a perfect day for a walk around the trails in the morning sun." Leon left just after them to drive off back towards Queens, to collect Andy and then Gino.

On their walk, news of Angie's boy and his new twin brother had buzzed ahead around the group, and she and Jeannette arrived, feeling like they had a bit of star status, with everyone wanting to hear how it all came about, and any news updates.

A friend from the walking group dropped Angie and Jeannette off back at the house, and they shared a coffee and talked through the situation, and how Brenda must be feeling. Angie thought back to when she adopted, and remembered how she found it hard to understand how anyone could bear having a baby taken away.

"Gino was so precious, and I'd not even given birth to him. But thinking back to when he was tiny, even the thought of losing him, or being taken away would keep me awake at night. I think I recall even then, thinking about how the woman - or girl - that gave birth to him, could bear having that perfect little boy just taken."

"Yes, I know, I remember having that same thought. I was eternally grateful to her of course and selfishly, very glad that she had. It struck home what she'd done for me, when I myself had Leon. There's an intensity in the bond in that first month or so, even more than when we adopted Andrew. It was then that I really got it. So much so that I've lit a candle for her - every 3rd of August!"

"Oh my, Jeannette, so have I - on Gino's birthday, every year - oh how very..." she tailed off, "that's such a coincidence - but understandable for us I guess." She pointed to the sky and they both watched a hawk circling overhead. "Looks like someone else searching for his lunch up there."

Leon had a quiet drive down to Queens, to collect them both with very little traffic, calling for Andy first. "Nice area this Andy, looks like a commuter belt kind of place."

"Yes it is, and a real mix - like me!" Andy joked, "with a lot of families around here from the Philippines, so there's plenty of South East Asian food in the grocery stores around here."

Leon took a left into Gino's street in Astoria - where he was already waiting for them on the sidewalk. On the drive out to Mom's, the boys talked through this morning's messages, and thoughts on when they might go over to Dublin. Andy smiled as he suggested they should book with Aer Lingus in honour of the mother country.

He noticed that Sinead had added another message he'd not seen in the group: 'that would be so lovely. I'm going over to see Mam again tomorrow after work anyway, so will ask her what she thinks about it too.'

"That would be amazing Andy - we'll have to see what she says. Have you got vacation left to take? I know you said you were over there earlier in the year."

"Yes, I should have, I'll check my calendar. I'm thinking we should go as soon as. How about you?" as he checked his phone calendar, "we could make it after Mum and Leon go back home on the Thursday. Looks like I can manage end of the week, and make it a long weekend if that works for you."

"Should do, I am pretty flexible this week - and the weekend could be long enough for a first visit." They arrived into Glen Cove at last, pulling up in front of the house.

Angie heard a sound from the road outside, "Is that the car pulling up out front? Sounds like our boys coming back" they smiled together. "I'm thinking we're about an hour to the sauce being properly ready. We should all sit on the terrace and have some of that delicious lemonade you made earlier; it should be nice and chilled by now."

Jeannette collected the jug from the refrigerator, and Angie carried a tray of glasses outside into the sunshine. Such a special time of real warmth, she thought - both from the sunshine and from the love for their families together.

"Hi Mom - hey, what's this - Old fashioned lemonade?"

"Absolutely - and we have Jeannette to thank for it."

"Hey mom - we've got another news flash for the 'lost twins podcast'" he laughed, "Andy messaged last night in our WhatsApp group about the idea of us going over to meet them - and Niall thinks 'that would be a grand idea'," in his attempt at an Irish lilt.

Jeannette clapped her hands together, "Oh that's super! Yes, it is a great idea - so you can actually meet those people who look a bit like you two. Your half sister and brother."

"...and three more sisters Mum. In spite of us dropping this emotional bombshell on her family, Sinead - and all of them, seem to have got used to the idea of us appearing, pretty quickly. It's totally amazing really - even that first Zoom call we had was only a week after my first message to her."

"Yeah - like Andy said, 'we just seemed to click'. A bit like the two of us I guess, eh? We're thinking of going over really soon - maybe this coming week if the timing works for Sinead."

"Well, I think this all sounds so wonderful. Such an exciting new chapter - for all of us I guess. Jeannette, do you want to come and help with the gravy while these boys chat?

"Such a gorgeous rich aroma Angie. We do long braising at home for the cheap tasty cuts, but it's usually very simple, with carrots and things like that. This smells so delicious."

The two mothers dished up the first course of fettuccine with some of the sauce and Leon looked up, "Angie, this is totally amazing,"

"Aw, thanks Leon. Like I told Andy, it's Nonna's recipe - Jeannette and I just added the time and the love," she smiled.

"You sell yourself short Angie. And just wait til the next course Leon, you'll love that,"

"So right, Andy," said Gino, bringing the salads to the table.

Over lunch, the two mothers told the boys of their morning walk, "It was so lovely walking through the woods and looking out across the sea from the walkway. Her friends were so lovely and really interested in our story."

"Oh, yes indeed, my walking group ladies were loving all our news about you boys. We've both got ourselves a bit of celebrity status and they loved having a real English lady as the star guest today," she laughed.

"I felt quite honoured, I must say. And we saw some fascinating information boards around there as well, telling about the Native tribes that used to live there. And Angie was saying so many place names here are tribal names - even Manhattan!"

"You're loving this aren't you Mum?" Andy smiled, "I'm so pleased you two are enjoying each other's company."

"We're *both* absolutely loving it, Andrew. And we do of course have quite a bit in common as you said! But yes, we really do get on well together. Leon's taking us on another day trip tomorrow to see Philadelphia."

"That sounds quite a journey."

"Looks like it will be OK, depending on the traffic of course, via the Verrazano bridge."

"I just have to show her the Liberty Bell - celebrate kicking you Brits out of America. I'd wanted to get there early enough to catch the Wanamaker Organ, but Macy's has closed there now. They used to play it every day at noon, so that's sad - but I read that they're trying to do something else with the place to make it more of a music venue. But there's plenty more to see there. We'll see what we can buy in the market there from the Amish guys - there's an amazing cheese stall there."

"Sounds like a long way to go for cheese?"

"No Andy, it's only a coupl'a hours down there but it should be a fun day. We might be able to stop off at Rutgers Gardens on the way back if there's time. Then we're both coming over to Manhattan with Leon on Tuesday to do the sights - and Gino suggested lunch somewhere nice."

"Oh yes, I can't wait, Angie. 42nd Street, Broadway, Central Park and all of that. And it would be lovely to see you boys for lunch."

"Sure will, Jeannette, I'll pick us somewhere nice and book it for the five of us. And I've a special treat lined up later. We're going to re-run our first meeting in Dillon's Irish pub - exactly one month on. I'd hoped to have them over to update them over dinner but we're all too busy. Max and Michelle will be there as well - and I'm sure Denny won't want to miss it, eh Andy?"

"Yes, I know it's hard to believe it but it's just four weeks - one month since our first meeting in there. So bizarre! So much seems to have happened to me - or to us - and to both of you mums. I hope you're enjoying the show Leon,"

"Ha, absolutely bro - it has been quite some ride!"

"And it will be swell to see Max again, it's been a while - and to thank him personally for starting all this off."

In the evening, Leon drove them back to Queens, discussing the events of the day. Gino remarked that the two brothers seemed to be really close - not quite the picture of sibling rivalry that Andy had painted.

"You know, I think you're right there. Andy and I did always have this kind of undercurrent when we were younger. Maybe it's something to do with us not spending as much time together recently but I don't know... It's really great seeing you two together as well, it's like, you seem different somehow bro. That thing about finding the other twin maybe? - the other half of you."

"Yeah, we've read a bit about that - there's a logic to it that makes it an interesting idea - but we're still not too sure how it works. I suppose I do feel different somehow - can't put a finger on it. But, think about it, only a month ago I didn't know Gino existed, and..."

"...and now, as Michelle said, we're finishing each others' sentences." they both laughed, "but, hey I guess it could be a thing. I know I never usually made friends, built relationships that easily. But here, it feels so different - like I just slipped into another mode, almost. We just 'click' as Andy puts it and it feels so natural."

"For me, looking from outside almost, I'd swear that you'd known each other for years, it's uncanny. Looking in the mirror here, it's even weirder - your two faces behind me!" he laughed, "I'm on chauffeur duty again tomorrow bro, down to

Philadelphia. You've barely driven this car since you picked us up."

"Yeah that was the idea. I can't park anything this size outside the apartment. I never really need a car anyway - subway and UBER does it all. I hope you all have a great day down in Philly tomorrow."

"And make sure you have a cheese steak for us."

19

Tuesday - Mum in Manhattan

Another Tuesday morning, though Andy knew that this was going to be a bit different - not just another Tuesday, as he took the subway into Manhattan from Woodside. Emerging into the daylight at 42nd and Bryant, he took his morning stroll through Bryant Park, on his route to The Packsmiths design studios - mentally comparing it to his life two years ago, in South London - or even to four weeks ago. That was before his life changed completely.

It was another crisp bright morning, and he saw some of the familiar faces of people meeting up - some on their cooling down jogs, or doing stretches after their morning run - others sharing a kiss before going their separate ways to offices nearby. He stopped as ever at the Italian coffee stand for a Macchiato and a little gift box, and looked up while he waited, enjoying the way the breeze was making the trees sway overhead.

As he waited to cross over on the way down to 37th, he looked up, thinking over the events over the last four weeks since Max had called out to him - just four weeks!

So much had happened. He ran through the chain of events in his mind, dwelling on that moment when Gino and Max came into Dillon's bar and seeing a… a sharper dressed version of himself - same hair colour - same face. What Leon was saying the last evening about how he had changed - and the way he and Gino were together; it is pretty weird when you stand back and think about it.

He felt his phone buzz and Sinead's WhatsApp said 'Mam would dearly love to meet you both. She cannot wait - she said,

"It's been too long coming", so let me know when you're thinking of'.

Gino was straight back while Andy was still reading it, 'We'll check our schedules Sinead, and yeah we're keen to meet up asap'.

Andy smiled at what he was thinking on the way in, how amazing it was how connected they were, as he crossed over 5th Avenue.

Leaving the elevator, he greeted Serena and handed her the box, "Here's those Cannoli I promised you,"

"Oh wow Andy, thanks so much. These look amazing - and like a couple of inches on my hips! I'm going to have to share them," she laughed, "You've certainly taken it to heart, having an Italian twin."

"I'm sinking in fast - even had Sunday Gravy at the weekend with Gino's mom." he smiled, "but anyway it's turned out that I'm Irish - at least genetically - so maybe I'll have to develop a taste for Irish Stew instead," he gave her a quick update on his twin and the new Irish family. "Catch you later."

He greeted Denny - who as usual was in the office first - finishing off a breakfast bagel. "I'm shooting out to meet Mum for lunch - Gino's gone and booked Le Rock - on his tab! But are you still on for this evening at Dillon's?"

"I wouldn't miss it, bud. Will be great to meet your family - families," he smiled.

The morning passed quickly, with a few simple jobs and a fair bit of admin, moving old projects onto the Archive server, before leaving for lunch. Andy walked south on 6th Avenue past Bryant again and into the Rockefeller centre - and waved at Gino, who'd managed to reserve one of the outdoor tables at the restaurant. "Pushing the boat out aren't you?"

Gino laughed, "ha ha, love your old country quaintness - but hell, yeah not the cheapest lunch Diner is it? But it's not every day you celebrate knowing a twin brother for a whole month!"

"Are you sure we can't go halves on it - it is a joint celebration."

"You can cover tonight at Dillon's if that would make up for it, but I really want to do this for you and your family. They both made the effort to come over here, and you know how much this all means to me, yeah?"

"OK, that's a deal then." He spotted their mums coming out to the table, "Hi Mum, hi Angie - or should I say Mums?"

"Hello darling. How was your morning? Hark at me - still being a Mum. Didn't we see the Rockefeller just earlier, from the Empire State, Angie?"

"Sure we did, along with the rest of the skyline," Angie smiled, "and Andy, we're only two of your mothers - you both have three 'Mums' now remember!"

"And we just heard back earlier from Sinead that our other 'mum' can't wait to meet us," Gino chipped in, "Andy's going to be booking flights later on, so we will be going over there almost straight after you fly back. We just need to sort out the details with Sinead."

Angie shook her head, "I can't believe how fast all this is going, son"

Lunch in Le Rock was a lovely experience, made more special by being al fresco in the late spring sun, with the towers of the Rockefeller around them.

"Gino, I must say, you've really made this one month celebration a special one." Jeannette looked a bit emotional almost, "What a beautiful place for lunch - and everyone's plate looked like a work of art almost. And Angie, I'm very much looking forward to thanking Max too later on - as he's the one responsible for these two finding each other in the first place - which of course, led to me getting to know you. I really feel I've found a kindred spirit - this truly has been such a special week. And while I'm on saying it, I can never thank you enough for your hospitality to Leon and me."

"This has been entirely my pleasure Jeannette. It's been so great getting to know you and Andy - and to teach you to cook Italian," she smiled, "it's like my family has just grown."

Walking into Central Park, the two mothers continued their conversation as Leon followed on, contributing now and then as they watched the skaters on the ice rink. But this was their time together as they continued on their walk through the park towards the Met, another of Jeannette's must-see places.

The park was busy that afternoon with runners and cyclists as well as other visitors enjoying the paths through the trees. As they strolled on, Jeannette thought much more interesting than the flat expanse of London's Hyde Park, and they paused as they rounded a bend in the footpath, to listen to a random jazz trio playing under a tree. Walking past the pond, they spotted a couple of model sailing boats tacking into a gentle headwind, just as Andy had mentioned.

It was hard to believe that it was only weeks since they first met in that Irish bar - which led to her walking with Angie through Central Park in the early summer sunshine. It will be fun to see the pub for themselves this evening, and to meet the Max that started all this. Their friends could also get the latest episode of the 'lost twin's podcast' live and straight from the horse's mouth, as it were.

20

The Monthiversary

They'd planned to all meet up again around 6, outside Peter Dillon's pub, after the mothers' sightseeing day in Manhattan. Andy arrived first with Denny chatting about the day's work, and only waited a couple of minutes before Gino appeared, "hey Denny, how's it going?"

"Real good - this will be quite an evening, eh bud? I'm looking forward to meeting your moms, guys."

Angie and Jeannette appeared a few minutes later, with Leon in tow. She laughed as they walked in, "This is more like it, Gino - a proper English pub!" as they moved inside.

"Ha ha, yeah, there are a few outposts of the old Empire over here. And - this was where it all started Jeannette. I walked in here just like this - with Max, there," as he gestured to his old friend, who was already sat at the barrel table in the centre with Michelle, "we saw Andy stood there - and we both just froze!"

"Yeah, you can imagine - we just stood looking at Andy for… seemed like forever. I thought it was weird when I saw him that morning - he looked like Gino, but a bit - er," smiling at Andy, "less groomed!"

Andy laughed, "and I had no clue who you were, or who Gino might be - until you both walked in here. It has certainly been a hell of a ride since then!"

Leon pretended to look shocked at Andy, "But what were you doing in here, the place is a temple to a dodgy Northern team, bro! It's all Newcastle United and 'Toon Army'. What would our Dad say? The big Chelsea fan would be so worried about you."

Andy and Leon both laughed, "I come in here now and then with Denny, as it's close to the office. The Chelsea pub is across town. Let's get the drinks in."

"Well, Leon," Jeannette smiled, "I'll not let on to him if you don't. I saw him last week, he's been fascinated by what's happened - and Andrew you must keep him up to date as well. And Michelle, how cruel of Max - not telling you about these two till you walked in and saw them!"

"I know, but I guess they were right - I really did get the same shock they'd both had at that first meet up."

Once the drinks arrived, Jeannette was talking to Michelle, as the music changed from the usual Irish folk background sound in the place, to a tune from the Hot House Flowers. They chatted about the music and found they both had a love of Jazz. Both had caught the bug from their fathers, Michelle told her she often went to a couple of clubs downtown, "I love some of the new guys that are coming in like Allan Bezama, Pasquale Grasso and Oscar Peñas."

"I know that Andrew used to go to Alfie's Jazz Club in Soho as well - less touristy than Ronnie Scotts. I think he's into jazz guitar as well. We both saw Danny Piers a while back, when he was last in London."

Michelle said, turning to Andy "Oh really. Hey, I didn't know you liked jazz, Andy. So we've more in common than just your twin brother," they laughed.

The mothers and their friends shared their thoughts on the next steps the boys were to take. The visit to actually meet their birth mother will be a real emotional roller coaster. Andy and Gino were talking that over as Max came over, "When are you two going to Dublin then?"

"Andy's booked us on the Thursday overnight on Aer Lingus, so will be there Friday morning."

Michelle smiled, "Hey, cool - flying Irish into Ireland, eh? Nice touch guys."

"That's what we were thinking. The Irish WhatsApp group has been buzzing today - I think Sinead is more than just a bit excited, eh Gino?"

"And how! And it sounds like Brenda - or should I call her 'Mammy' - is too. Sinead was telling us how she seems like a changed woman. All those years of living with that sense of shame, I guess. That's how she, and all those other women were made to feel by the nuns - and the system. Andy's been reading about all this Magdalene Laundry scandal, and it sounds like many of the women had been kept in almost slave labor conditions, some of them for years; completely broken. I guess Brenda was lucky to get out of the system and get a job."

"...and forty years later, you two turn up - like bad pennies!" Denny jibed.

Michelle joined them leaving the two mothers to talk, "Did I hear you say you're going over this week, Gino?"

"Sure did, Andy's booked the flights for the Thursday overnight."

"How do you both feel about it - excited or maybe a bit mixed?"

"Yeah - sure will be almost a step into the unknown, though as Andy was saying before, Sinead and Niall have gone from being real wary in those early messages, to talking to us like we're really close."

"...and from what Sinead has told us, Brenda sounds like she's so excited she can't wait to see us - again!"

Michelle laughed, "Yes, forty plus years later. But I'd guess - speaking from a position of me not being a mother - having given birth to you, she must have a huge emotional hole to fill. I know from my own mom looking for her sibling, that Grandma got real emotional - mixed feelings I think. She didn't want her little girl, Kim - as she named her - to have lived with feeling rejected by her. And on the flip side, she didn't want to feel rejected herself, if Kim didn't want any contact. It's a tough one."

"Oh yeah, I hadn't factored that in, Gino. Brenda might have been thinking we blame her for abandoning us, or whatever - and I suppose might be a bit unsure of how we'll be."

"We'll have to make sure Sinead lets her know not to stress over that. Can't wait to meet her, that's some life she's lived, and it will be great to be there - for her."

Angie came over to the boys, "Jeannette just had a thought of us two going over to meet Brenda maybe, as well sometime. Is that something you could bring up with Sinead when you see her? See how they'd feel about that?"

"We would just love to say thanks to her for you two boys - in person. After all, she gave us the best gift in the world - our families."

"Oh, Jeannette, that's such a sweet way to put it - you do have a way with words. You got me all tearful thinking about it!"

Michelle clapped her hands, "What a really great idea - you'll have to put that to them guys. My guess is that she would love to meet the two women who turned her babies into the fine men they are now." she chuckled.

"Yeah, you're right, they didn't turn out too bad," laughed Max.

Andy was thinking that this had been such a great idea, bringing their friends and families together, as they walked to the subway later, to go their separate ways. Leon had parked at the station out near Glen Cove again, so he and their mothers were off to Penn Station to pick up the LIRR.

There was a mess of them all hugging each other, to round the evening off perfectly. Gino called over to Andy, "Talk to you in the morning about the Dublin trip?"

"That works for me. Denny and I'll be out with a few guys from work tomorrow evening - agency drinks night at the 'Agency of Record'. So morning is best for me."

"That sounds like it could end up dangerous, Andy!"

"Ha ha, it often does for the young bucks - usually sales types - the BDMs. Out come the shots - and its tequila and testosterone fuelled mayhem. We go along to meet up with some of the others and talk design and pick up any client gossip. It's all about who's won what account, and who's moving agency, that kind of stuff. So I'll be the one with the clear head for Thursday to fly to Dublin!"

"Best idea on a weekday - but yeah, I'll call you at breakfast, when I'm up."

Mom's thoughts

"What an amazing day - and such a swell idea of the boys to take us to the place they met up - just four weeks ago! Oh my, so much has happened in those four weeks, it's hard to take it all in.

"A month ago I'd never heard of Andy - or Jeannette or Leon. I'd never met Michelle, though Gino had spoken about her a while back - what a lovely woman. And now - and now, it's like I've got this great big family. So many new names, I even feel close to Sinead, even though we've never spoken. She's my boy's half sister, so why shouldn't I feel close?

"I just love Jeannette's idea to go and meet Brenda and her family. That's of course if they want to meet us two - maybe the boys will be enough for them. They do sound like they are lovely folks, and seem to be welcoming our boys into their hearts.

"Oh, and that easy way Andy and my Gino are with each other, it's so good to see - talking together at breakfast and all - having only just met.

"I can't wait to hear how it all goes for them at the weekend - maybe another of those 'podcasts' the boys kept talking about - whatever they are!

"I just can't stop smiling to myself - and yes it really is so sad that Joe wasn't able to be a part of all this. I just want to go home and tell him all about it, like he's still just… there. I know he wasn't the most emotional type of guy, but he would have been so excited for our Gino, same as I am."

21

Planning for Dublin

Breakfast phone calls had become a bit of a fixture for Andy and Gino, with so many things happening. Wednesday morning, they called to confirm the details of the flights to Dublin and the hotel. Andy suggested they book the Beaumont Hotel, which looked to be a few minutes away from Brenda's - Mam's house.

"That sounds OK, Andy - and the Tripadvisor reviews say it's decent, though you never know with that. Oh, and I saw the booking confirmation email from Aer Lingus - thanks - I'll transfer that over to you later."

"No rush - we can divvy it all up after the weekend, if that's easier."

"Hah, 'divvy' - love it man! Yeah, we'll have the hotel, taxis and plenty more to divvy, I'll bet ya. Hey, it's not a cheap hobby, finding two new families!" They both laugh at the idea. "So, you'll be joining Leon and your mom, dropping them off, and returning the hire car, before we fly?"

"Great, it's good the flights are not too far apart; they fly just after 8, and ours is just after 9. I'm meeting them at Jamaica station at 5 with my bags, to take them over to departures, so we can say goodbye properly. Then drop the car off, and meet you in T7 departures."

"You know this week has been really great, Mom has loved having Jeannette here, they've become real pals, I think."

"Absolutely. I know my Mum's loved it too - she said it's been a real treat getting to know you and her. They've had quite a time of it together going all over the place."

"It's drawn Mom out of herself a little - going places she's not been to since Dad passed, like those gardens and the Met. She'll have new memories of them now."

"That's great, I need to be off to work shortly. Catch you later anyway - we're talking with Sinead at breakfast tomorrow again, if that's OK. She messaged earlier - I guessed that would be OK with you."

"Sure - oh and keep off the shots tonight - we've a plane to catch tomorrow!"

The ride into work was same as ever - plugging into the latest 'Resourceful Designer' podcast episode, for the ride into Manhattan. He reflected on what Sinead had said the other day about the closeness of their family, more so than his own when growing up. Taking in the faces in his car, he turned to wondering about the people and all their stories; what drives them, and their families. In some ways he felt a bit jealous of them; that they knew exactly where they came from, and who they're connected to.

But was that his old self, thinking like that, maybe? His business connections have been growing quite a bit recently, and he and Gino certainly know a lot more about where he - or they both were from. The coming weekend was going to be interesting.

He realised he'd not actually heard a big chunk of the podcast - it had just become a background noise to his thoughts. Turning it off, he thought more about his own position - and Gino's really.

Legally his Grandma Carmine was his grandma, and his Mum was his mother and had brought him up with love. He shared no DNA, so he had no idea of things like a family medical history - but it's Mum and Dad who shaped him and made him who he is. Then again, there's obviously something there in the DNA - both he and Gino followed a design based career, despite being brought up in different environments.

Maybe meeting his birth mother and the family will help his thoughts gel a bit better. That was something else - being plucked from a mother, and what could have been a connected family, to one of having no back story. That's all changed. He was looking forward to finding out more about Sinead and Brenda's wider family too - and fitting all that into what he knew about himself, and his work life here in Manhattan.

He took his usual route through Bryant Park to pick up his regular Macchiato, to slip back into his work life for the rest of the day.

Early that evening, Andy and Denny chatted about current design jobs and the day's events, as they walked the few streets from the office, across Park Avenue to the Westin, where informal agency drinks were happening, sponsored by a leading ecommerce tech supplier, at the 'Agency of Record'. It was billed as a restaurant and bar to evoke the "golden era of advertising", with an impressive list of DJs and cocktails.

The notice at the entrance had proudly announced DJ Portamento being on the decks that evening and, as ever at these events, catching up with people was a lot about lip reading. There was a lot of talk about who had moved, or was moving to which new role - and a few hints that one of the big food brands was going out to pitch, after years at their own 'agency of record', ironically enough.

From Andy's point of view, that was less of a threat, as their own agency serviced many of the lead design houses with the packaging and POS stuff he was usually tied up with. So even if his biggest client were to move main agencies, he'd probably still get the packaging work - albeit with a new twist or concept.

They headed for the bar and bumped into one of their ex-colleagues who'd moved to a rival agency, and Denny had already fed part of Andy's story to him.

"So, Andy - I hear you've grown yourself a brand-new twin brother?"

"I have indeed, Jim - you've been talking to Denny, I guess?" Andy gave an abridged version of the story so far, with the meeting and all the DNA stuff to date, "and funnily enough, we were only talking the other day, and Denny suggested we set up a 'lost twins podcast'. So many people that Gino and I know, have only heard bits of the story."

"I'm not in the least bit surprised Andy, that is one hell of a tale."

"...and tomorrow we take the overnight to Dublin, to meet our Irish birth 'Mam'. So this really is an exciting part of the story. Next episode coming up," he announced, as they laughed.

"I can't wait to hear it man."

The evening conversation moved on to work related gossip, and who's dating who type conversations. Denny, Jim and Andy made their escape before the shots started doing the rounds, and they carried on chatting together as they made their way to the subway.

"Tomorrow's the day - I'll see you first thing Denny, but I'm leaving around 12. I need to pack, and then go out to Jamaica station to meet Mum and Leon, drop them off at the airport and take the rental back. So, there's a bit to do before I fly."

"OK, sure. So there'll be more for the next podcast instalment, eh?" he added. "G'night - and see you in the morning."

The subway back to Woodside was a lot quieter than the morning commute. Andy's mind drifted again, into wondering about the stories of each of the others on the train with him, something that wouldn't really have crossed his mind, just a few weeks ago. The twenty something couple sat looking just a bit disconnected, the guy hanging on the bars by the doors scrolling his phone, the elderly couple holding hands in contented companionship. Each had a unique story, building their own path through life.

But few can be as strange as his own story had become, over the last few weeks. He had added another complete back story, and his mental picture of who he was in life had changed completely.

He ran through all that had happened to him - to them both. The new friendships and Dillon's bar. He'd not often been for a beer there before, apart from a few times with Denny. His Manhattan haunt had usually been the Football Factory, the New York home of Chelsea FC, with a few acquaintances, with just football in common. Now, there in Dillon's, even the bar staff knew their story - or a small part of it anyway. And over recent weeks, it had become their meeting spot - 'the place where I first met my twin brother'.

That still sounded a strange concept, saying it to himself. He looked around to check if he'd actually said it out loud - and cracked a smile to himself.

—— 22 ——

Thursday & flying to Dublin

Time for another breakfast Zoom chat with Sinead - it was a convenient point in the day for both of them. With a cup of tea and breakfast in front of him, he opened the laptop and set up the session. Gino appeared straight away, and Sinead not far behind.

"G'Morning lads - my twin big brothers," she laughed, "that sounds so strange, to be sure! In your separate windows there, at least I can tell yous apart now - I think."

"Hah, I was thinking the same on the subway home last night Sinead, saying 'my twin brother' still takes a bit of getting used to."

"I've had a lot more chat with Mam, and I thought it would be good to bring you both up to speed, before you come over. This is all stuff we're just finding out new for ourselves, so we are. Mam is keen for yous both to know as well. It is kind of cathartic for her, I think. She's going through a mental cleansing almost."

Sinead fills them in on more background, on how her Mam and Da were childhood sweethearts in their village, just outside Waterford on the south coast. "It was a sweet relationship, like any young girl would want. Then Mammy told me and Niall about this family friend, Kevin Walsh, who was in fact the leader of the church youth group. He often invited her and her younger sisters over to play with his own daughters, who were actually both younger than her as well. It was all just friendly fun with the girls at the start.

"As she got older, she'd grown out of the games the younger girls were still playing together, as our mam was very much the big sister, and a bit more mature by then; Kevin was paying her

116

more and more attention it would seem. He was a bit of a local joker, a bit of an eejit, and the 'life and soul' type, and full of the craic, you know. That would concern - or maybe alarm me nowadays of course, with my own girls.

"Anyhow as she was becoming more of a teenager, he became more… physical with her and then it all went too far and he forced himself on her. Mammy said he'd interfered with her a few times before, 'play fighting' he called it - but then he raped her, it was just the once, when the play went too far. Of course, he put the fear of God into her not to tell, said 'no-one would believe any of this - I'd say you led me on', type of thing."

Andy nodded, "That sounds a well worn story,"

"Anyhow, nature took its course, so it did. So, yes, after a few months she started to show, and her Daddy, our granda, just would not believe her and blamed it on our Da, Michael, even though he'd been working on a cousin's farm over in Cork for most of the year. Then he told her it was her own fault for being promiscuous, wearing these short skirts, shouted at her and struck her - yes, struck her for 'bringing shame on our family'. So, yes, after that, and like with so many other women in Ireland it seems, the parish priest said he would arrange a mother and baby home for her - and she was shipped off to Dublin a few days after it all came out."

"Did nobody else challenge that?"

"Well, there's the shame in it all. The last thing anyone would do in a small village like that, would be to own up to the shame of their daughter, pregnant out of wedlock. Especially back then, so there was a story about getting a job and staying with a cousin in Dublin.

"Then you know quite a bit of the story from your own births, to her being locked up in the bloody laundry with those evil bastard nuns. How on God's earth they can describe themselves as being bloody Christians, I have no idea. What the hell was in their heads?"

"Hey, you've really got it in for the nuns that ran the place, Sinead."

"I've been doing a lot of reading about all this Magdalene scandal, Gino, since I found out about Mam being stuck in it, and it all just beggars belief. How on God's earth could sane, rational - and supposedly 'Christian' priests and nuns have devised such a vile, warped, and downright evil scheme?" Sinead railed, "The Magdalene that Mam was incarcerated in, was named the 'Our Lady of Charity and Refuge Convent' - what a bloody travesty - 'charity and refuge'? It was a haven of cruelty and slave labour," she was visibly shaking with anger.

"And to cap it all, would you believe, I just read that all the four orders of the nuns responsible for all this shameful activity - not the least of which was putting 10,000 women through hell - they have refused to contribute to the state fund for recompense. I've been reading a lot about all this since all our news came out - I'll share some of the links in the chat when I find them again. That fund was eventually set up to compensate the women who worked in them - the least they should do, based on their profits from the business."

"The Catholic church in this country is, is… pah!" She didn't need to finish the sentence.

"That's appalling, and yes I want to read it all about it."

"No problem Andy, I'll send it over. Anyhows, that's all off my chest now!" she sighed heavily, "so, practical stuff now, eh? So yous boys will be coming on Aer Lingus, I gather - what's the flight number, so I can check on it?"

"Sure Sinead. We're on EI106 - and we've booked rooms at the Beaumont, which looks to be not too far away."

"That's grand Andy. Not far from the airport or our Mam's. They do quite good food as well, so you'll be fine in there. Right, I'll check on the airline arrivals page in the morning, and meet you both there. I can't believe I'm going to meet yous both so soon - neither can our Mammy. We are thinking it best for yous to meet her on Saturday, if that's OK with you. Daddy's got a hospital appointment on the Friday, so we don't want to upset that."

Niall at last managed to get a word in, "Looking forward to meeting you both, and you have a safe flight."

After saying their goodbyes, Andy and Gino went off to work, Andy messaged Leon to confirm the time for him to get to the Jamaica station that afternoon to pick him up.

Another morning of shelf dressing artwork for Andy, for a range of potato based snacks. He'd designed the product packaging a while ago, from the lead agency's initial briefs, so this was his baby really, especially with the Manga characters he'd created and introduced to extend the concept. It was a world away from the much simpler projects he'd been working on in London.

On his way out to Jamaica station on the LIRR, he was thinking through the last jobs he remembered at the London agency - roller banners for a tyre fitters' reception, and a set of promotional brochures for a group of nursing homes. Not as much fun as today's work - but, he reminded himself, he got this job based on his portfolio of chutney labelling and promo materials that he'd designed in London, so it had been a useful stepping stone.

As it was, it had actually turned out to be a massive step - taking him to New York - taking him into a different world - taking him to a scenario where a stranger calls at him 'Hey, Gino!'. Yes, all this had become a big part of his developing back story now. The coming weekend would add more details again.

"Hey, Andy, we're over here." Leon broke into his reverie, waving at him as he came down the stairs from the tracks, "I managed to get parked around the corner here. I thought it best to book a space online. It looks a bit of a busy junction around here." They chatted about their mornings on their way over to the car. "Do you want to take over the driving?"

"Sure Leon, I'd better get some time behind the wheel, and I'll be dropping you both off soon anyway." He waved as they approached the car, "hi Mum, how was your Wednesday, I missed you. Gino said you'd been for a day out somewhere."

"I missed you too. We had a lot of fun. Angie took us over to a place called Fire Island, on the ferry, and we hired bikes there and went for a ride around. She said she'd not ridden for years, but we both managed quite well, didn't we, Leon?" as Andy drove off, into the traffic towards the airport.

"You did well, and yeah, it really was great - all pretty flat so no hills to climb."

"There were parts where we couldn't cycle. Some villages don't even allow bikes, so we had to get off and walk through them. A really different kind of America. Have you been there before, Andrew?" he shook his head, "it's really worth a trip out there. Cars are banned there, so it's really peaceful."

"There are mostly holiday homes from the look of it, so I'd guess it gets pretty busy when schools are out - but we found it pretty quiet. Angie had even packed a picnic lunch for us all, as well," Leon added.

"Oh yes! Such a treat - Angie had baked a focaccia that morning, which she'd sliced and added ham and salami, and some fresh fruit. So we had our lunch on the beach, which was lovely, then a beer in one of the cafes. We all rode off through woodlands overlooking the bay with just the sounds of wind and waves - well apart from the jet planes coming in to land of course!"

"That sounds really good fun, I'll have to check it out. I'm pleased you had a good last day."

Turning on to the expressway toward JFK, as he joined all the other airport traffic, his mind turned to the flight and what came next. Jeannette checked her passport for the umpteenth time, and Leon smiled at Andy, "It's not moved Mum."

"I know it will be there where I put it, but you know how I am."

Unloading their bags from the back of the Lincoln, Andy hugged them both, and waved, watching as they disappeared through the doors, into the terminal.

After dropping the car off at the rental office, Andy took the Airtrain back to Terminal 7, taking in the views of airport busyness, and wondering which plane Leon and his mum would be on.

Just like they'd planned, he'd found a seat in the departures area, near the Aer Lingus check in desk, when Gino came in from the Airtrain.

Gino smiled at Andy, as they checked in to drop off their bags, to fly to the 'auld country'! "I hope this lot are better than Delta - can't be any worse, I guess."

The ground crew clerk looked at them both, then down at the US and UK passports, then back up at them as she picked up the phone.

"Can you explain this to me please, gentlemen?" Andy and Gino looked at each other, and laughed.

"I'm sorry - that really must look confusing," Andy apologised, "we were actually both adopted as babies, and have just recently found each other again."

"Oh my word, so you are actual twins then?" she asked, putting the phone back down, "how does that happen? You're British right?"

Gino picked up the story, and gave a short version of how they discovered each other, as she looked on, wide eyed, "Oh man what a story that is - you guys should tell it on that TV show! That sure is some tale. I was about to call Homeland Security when I checked your passports," she laughed. "Well, you boys have a wonderful time over there meeting your new 'Mam'. Safe trip to you both," as she handed them their boarding cards.

They both laughed as they walked off to the security and departures, comparing their passports, "I'm sure that's going to happen a lot on this trip."

"Oh, and I didn't tell you this - it may be easier coming the other way. The best part of flying Aer Lingus," Andy added, "will be coming back, as we go through US immigration in Dublin. Makes it so much quicker than joining the lines coming back into JFK."

"That sounds like a great idea!"

Security and Departures went through reasonably quickly and they settled down with a beer to watch the sea of people in the terminal. Andy shared how his subway ride had changed recently, "I've taken to looking at people around me in the car and wondering about their story - their families. Other people have a firm 'back story' I call it - they know where they're from and what to expect from life. Do you know what I mean?"

"I think so. So are you thinking we don't?"

"I got to thinking that we didn't know anything from before - these people all have aunts and grandads in the family that look like them. I'm almost jealous, I think. Is that weird?"

"No, it's like we both told our moms, it's having someone that looks like us. We've both gone through a lot of soul searching, I guess - maybe you're just a bit more sensitive to all that. Well, this weekend should help us both get to know more of our back stories, I guess."

They finished their beers, and headed off to the gate where EI106 was boarding.

Friday in Dublin

As the plane descended from their overnight flight and the cabin lights came up, the boys saw very little of their approach before landing in Dublin just after 8.30, emerging through the low cloud cover - and the usual airport buildings and hangars appeared only minutes before touchdown.

Sinead would be meeting them at the airport and they were both looking forward to seeing her at last in real life.

As they came out of the baggage collection, they spotted Sinead, even before they saw the card she'd written with their names, and they both rushed over to meet her with a group hug, "Ah you yanks, you're all so touchy feely!" she laughed.

"Just him Sinead, I'm the reserved one from England."

"Surely you lot are just as bad, so you've no excuses there," they laughed. "Dear God, it's so wonderful to see you both - in real life - I feel I know yous so well already, though I must say, you're both a lot taller than you look on Zoom!"

"So great to finally meet you too, Sinead," said Gino, smiling as they walked out towards the car park, "you know when we started all this, we were worried that you may want nothing to do with us, dropping that bombshell into your family like that."

"Not a bit of it. Well, maybe there was just a bit at the start. It was just such a massive shock, I didn't know where you were coming from, at the time, Andy. I re-read it and asked myself what kind of scam it was, so I did! While I was waiting there for you to arrive just earlier, I re-read my reply to the first message you sent in the app, from way back, though it wasn't actually that long ago. I could see that I hadn't a clue what I was about to learn… and was about to happen to us all."

"I know, we had no idea where it would lead us, Sinead - and sorry we didn't tell you about Gino as well, at the start."

"No, I totally get why it made sense to do it that way. But then, when it all came out, and Mammy told us about the twin babies and poured her story out - it was just wonderful that it was both of you that had searched and found us - and more than that, it's been so wonderful for Mammy. She's really come out of herself - that weight off her shoulders, like a release - she's almost a changed person, as I said on the call."

Sinead worked her way through the airport exit roads, turning South on to Swords Road. "Now, your hotel is not far from here in Beaumont, that should be only a few minutes away depending upon the roads, of course. Mammy lives on this side of the City, so we'll not have to work through all that Dublin traffic."

"Sounds good, Sinead - and we're meeting your mam tomorrow?"

"Yes - I wasn't sure how jetlagged you'd be, so I thought if you want to check in, we could have a coffee in the bar - unless you're wanting to get some shuteye?"

"I'll be fine, as I slept a bit on the plane, how about you Gino?"

"All good here too - we can drop our bags and join you for coffee."

"Ah good, in which case, Niall said he'd be able to join us for lunch, if you're up for that, and then maybe head into town?"

"That will be great too, it will be good to meet him too. At the hotel, or somewhere else?"

"The food there's pretty good as I said, so yous won't have to go far. I'll let him know." Sinead pulled up and dropped them at the door and went off to park the car.

Over coffee, Sinead talked them through her Dad's hospital visit diagnosis. Mam wanted the rest of that day to be simple, and not too confusing for him. He's not too bad at the moment, though he knows about your visit, and what it means for Mam."

Over coffee, the conversation moved on, as Sinead asked, "I realised the other day that I've no idea what yous both do for a living. I know you moved to New York for work and did you say you're a designer?"

"Yes, I'm at an agency that designs artwork for packaging, in-store promotions and all that goes with it."

"So you're an artistic one, same as me?"

"Ah, right. And so's Gino here - he's got an interior design and remodelling company. Sounds like it's something in the genes maybe."

"That makes the 'company' sound a bit bigger than it is man, but yeah it is. We set it up with some backing from my dad, who was in construction. How about you, what do you do, Sinead?"

"I myself took a fine art degree, then I started with a job out of college, as a gallery assistant in the National Gallery of Ireland."

"That sounds like a good first career step."

"Well, it was in part Andy. I loved painting and printmaking particularly, but that's a precarious living to be had, so it had to be a boring admin job for practicality. The degree had proved that I loved art I suppose, and maybe that's what got me the job. It was a lot of admin, then just moving pictures about, liaising with other galleries, and then helping with special exhibitions coming in."

"So you're not still there then?"

"No, I'm now assistant curator in a commercial gallery Gino - a dream job really - a big two story gallery, mostly dealing with contemporary Irish artists. Really dynamic environment, and helping to give visibility to some exciting new painters and sculptors."

"That sounds great. So the art scene is strong here from the sound of it."

"Absolutely Gino, maybes not on the level of New York, I'll say, but we do all right," she smiled, "so we all share artistic genes certainly, my - our Great Grandad Patrick was a signwriter down in Waterford. There's still a few bars there with the signs that he painted."

"That's cool - and I'd love to see your gallery Sinead. And we told you Andy has Patrick as a middle name?"

"Yes, I remember you saying. Well, if you're not busy this afternoon, perhaps we could take a spin into town after lunch, park at the gallery, and then maybe show you some of the sights as well?"

"Great idea - ah, Sinead - this tall guy must be Niall," they all got up as he strode into the lounge.

"What's the craic? Gino - Andy," Niall smiled, and looked searchingly from one to the other.

"That's Andy - messy hair," Gino laughed, and shook hands with Niall.

"No no, Gino, that's just the relaxed look - and I'd know yous lads anywhere," he laughed, pointing at his own chin, "well, welcome to Dublin. I'll guess Sinead's been putting yous both in the picture, on the latest Mammy's been sharing with us, so."

"I'll say," Andy nodded, "fascinating in part, and heart rending for most of it. It has not been easy to take on board - and even more so probably for you all."

"Welcome to our new world, lads," Sinead looked at each of them, "we're all learning about it all together. There's been quite a bit of coverage of all this laundry business since the scandal broke, and there's still a few articles that come up in the news about it all, now and then, though I'm pretty sure the Church is trying its damnedest to stop them being published."

After they'd ordered food, Niall added, "So Sinead's right on that, and that Cillian Murphy has brought the issue back into the mainstream, with that new film he made. I think it's called 'Small Things Like This', or something like that. When a big star like that tackles the subject - he called it 'a collective trauma' I think, which it certainly is - it can only help in keeping it all in the public eye."

"We thought we might cause a few problems, us turning up like that after 40 years, and turning your lives upside down. But it sounds like it's not been all bad though."

"To be sure Andy, it was a long time coming, just as Mammy said. And Sinead said this, I think it's been almost a healing process for her. More important for her, she'll be able to reconnect with you."

"Exactly what I said, Niall." They talked the boys through more of the family history, down in Waterford; and how there'd not been a great deal of contact or love from the grandparents,

126

understandably. "Mam had taken us children down there, out of duty when we were older, but it was obvious that Dad was avoiding them, as he'd rarely join us 'because of work', he said and even when he did, he didn't talk to grandad. We'd never really noticed - but after hearing all this, it all seems obvious to us now, so it does."

After lunch, Niall went off back to work. Sinead took them into Dublin, and along Sean Mac Dermott Street, pointing out the Magdalene building, "that's the place. The place where it all began. It's being set up now as a centre for remembrance," as she slowed and pulled the car into a space, and they looked out at the forbidding looking building and its solid green door.

"That makes it feel more… real - and jeez! How real."

"…and overlaying our mam's story - it's so hard to imagine how a society tolerated it."

"I know - but this was a big red light district way back when, so I suppose folks felt it was doing a good service. I've come around here a few times since Mam started sharing her story. It chills me every time."

They drove off and she parked easily at the back of the gallery. They went inside through the loading doors, and Sinead led them into the gallery space, "Hey, Seán. What about you? These are my twin brothers I've been telling you about."

"Well, well, well, how really great to meet you both. I feel I already know so much about you, with all that Sinead has told me about yous."

"Good to meet you too, this is quite some place you have here," Gino scanned the paintings on the wall opposite, "there's some amazing work - and I love these two, like next generation Rothkos almost, but more vibrant."

"That's Sean Scully - Turner prize nominee a few times, I think," Seán offered, "we held a retrospective in our upper gallery a while back. These are a couple he painted about 10 years ago I think, we're lucky to have them to show - and sell of course. So I guess you have the same artsy genes Sinead is blessed with?"

Andy smiled, "We're both a little bit - Gino's an interior designer and remodels stylish Manhattan apartments - and I'm a graphic designer. So, there must be something in it - it can only be the genes I suppose, as nothing else influenced us. I was lucky in getting a bursary to Croydon College of Art to study fine art and graphics, to take it further, and ended up in commercial graphic design."

"Well, well, there's the coincidence - times two, I think," Seán said, "I was there myself in '92 - and so, if I'm not mistaken, was our Sean Scully here - though a lot earlier. There's been a lot of talent thorough that college!"

After the tour of the gallery, Sinead took them out onto St Anns Street, and off for a walking tour, to see some of the sights of the City, "I'll take a guess that after sitting on a plane for all that time, a chance to stretch your legs would be welcome. We'll take a walk by Dublin Castle, and then on to Temple Bar, which should give the flavour of the city for yous."

"Yeah, that's a great idea, we've done a load of sitting around - airports - on the plane - hotel. Gino said he's not been here before, and I've only seen the inside of the bars here on a stag weekend a while back, so it will be good to see it properly."

"OK - let's do it!"

The afternoon stroll gave them the chance to talk more about their lives, and the boys shared the events of last week, with their mothers spending time together on Long Island. Their walk took in the castle, Temple Bar area, stopping off at a bar beside the river for a drop of the black stuff - "well it would be rude not to," as Andy said. Then alongside the Liffey, and back past the University towards the Gallery and Sinead's car.

"Now do you guys want to get back to the Beaumont - or maybe stay around here, and get a cab back later on? I've got my girls to deal with."

"Shall we stay here, Andy?" Andy gave a thumbs up, "That's cool with us Sinead - probably more life around here than at a suburban hotel for the evening." Gino laughed.

"...and I thought I spied a comedy club back in Temple Bar, I think it was. That could be good. We'll not have too many beers as we've an important date tomorrow morning."

"You certainly have boys. Have a good evening and I'll pick yous up from the Beaumont at 10."

Tomorrow they'd meet the woman who gave birth to them - gave them life.

Mam's thoughts

"Well I never thought I'd ever see the day. I'd held out no hopes for even knowing what happened to them only a week or two since. When I first told Michael about them after we met up again, he was sure they'd been put up for adoption, and disappeared well before he found me.

"Those sweet faces - That photo of those two boys, with a look of my own Daddy, and Niall of course - such wonderful looking young men, it makes my heart burst. I so thank the Lord that they've not taken a look of that Kevin Walsh, not at all, as far as I can see.

"All that pain - all that hurt - I thought I'd take that all to my grave but this… It's like a whole new chapter. I hope Michael takes it all in as well; he remembers all the anguish back at home - and then him finding me in Dublin and encouraging me to feel better about myself - and then our marriage, and the children. What a special man he is.

"I wonder what these boys will be like to talk to. Sinead tells me they're lovely chaps and they had a grand day today - who'd have thought? An Englishman and an American, ha. My Michael will love that - he'd always wanted to go over there. I wonder if…

"Oh, I'm not sure I'll sleep tonight, my head's just buzzing!"

— 24 —

Meeting Brenda

Sinead had arranged to collect them from the Beaumont after breakfast on Saturday, 'Mammy couldn't wait any longer to meet you both,' she'd told them on WhatsApp. They drove off, and it was only a few minutes before they arrived outside a neat looking semi-detached house, with cream painted render upstairs, similar to rows of others they'd passed on the way into the estate - and Niall was there, stood in the front garden, watching for them.

"How's things lads, Gino, Andy!"

The twin brothers greeted Niall again, in another group hug, as Andy spied Brenda through the front window, "and I take it this lady here is your mother?"

"She surely is - or should we say our mother - our Mam - and I take it those flowers are intended for her?" as he moved to go inside, "Hey, Sinead, we should all go indoors, and not give the neighbours too much more to gawp at?"

Sinead laughed, "Come on inside you two - Mammy's dying to meet yous both. We'll have a day of it. I'll be making some sandwiches, while you two have some time with Mam. Then our sisters will be along later on to meet you."

Brenda, with a huge smile on her face, was standing beside the fireplace in the lounge as they walked in. A huge smile, but you could almost feel the forty years of pain. Forty years of just… not knowing there as an undercurrent… and them appearing back in her life was helping to start and wash them away.

Those twin boys - her twin boys - were there again. She came across and held them in one of the most heartfelt hugs of her life. It was a strange meeting in some ways, with both lads being so

130

aware of how much this meant to her. So much of what she had kept hidden away from everyone for most of her life, was now out there and known by all her children - including themselves, the two 'new additions' to her family.

She was finding it difficult to actually say anything to Andy and Gino - so they just held her in a hug. "I guess there's no need for words right now - er… Mam," to which they all laughed, pulling away to just look at each other.

"Well it's just so… you know. I've spent my life not knowing - and here yous both are," she smiled warmly letting it wash over her, just looking from one to the other, moist eyed, and touching their cheeks, "and thank you both so much for those beautiful flowers. Seems like you've been brought up right, so it does," she said with a glint in her eye.

Brenda settled in her chair, as Sinead brought in a tray of tea for them. Mam asked them about their lives in London and New York, and their chance meeting only a few weeks ago when they discovered each other. "I know I've heard this all already from Sinead here, I just want to hear it all over again from yourselves."

She smiled, leaning forward as she soaked up the story of how all their friends had got so involved and excited for them as their search progressed - and at hearing how they had just clicked and accepted each other, without question. Gino shook his head, "you know, we've been talking about this a lot, and it never crossed my mind to not… not… become closer to Andy,"

"…especially when our DNA result was so conclusive that we are twins. It just felt so natural to both of us."

"Yous have no idea how happy that makes me," she paused to take it all in, "You know, I've been picturing in my mind all these years, thinking where you both were, and what you were doing, leading your own lives. Imagining yous going through school, or what you might be doing - always thinking you had to be somewhere near Dublin and always together. I was always looking out for twins when I was out around the shops. Not a bit of it was even close to what you were actually up to." she gently shook her head, smiling sadly.

She then told them more about her own life, growing up in Waterford, playing in the fields round about the village, "that might sound like a kind of rural idyll, though of course, life was not that easy for us - money was always tight. Well it was for all of us back then, so it was. Our house was small for the five of us, but it was in a nice spot on the village outskirts, and looked out over the River Suir where I played out with my sisters. And then… Sinead said she told you how I fell pregnant with the two of yous, and the way that all came about?" They both nodded.

"Well, that Kevin Walsh had been a family friend since we were young - he led the church youth group, as you know, so was a bit of a leading light. My little sisters were school chums with his own girls. He himself was a real charmer, and I guess I got drawn in with all the compliments, saying things like, 'my, you've become such a beautiful young woman' and 'you're the prettiest girl in the village here now, I'll bet you've got boys running after you'," she let her gaze wander out of the window, as she went over it all in her mind.

"Well, I became quite used to being puffed up like that, as any young girl would; though I was not so keen on him slipping his arm around me, even while we were sat watching my sisters playing as well. He'd stroke my waist or my arm. I told him I had a boyfriend - which he knew anyway - and that I didn't need cuddling, to which he laughed, and asked me 'why's he run away to Cork then?'

"Over time he got even more 'playful', he called it. Then one afternoon I went round to collect my sisters, but his wife Marie had taken them down to the local playground with their own girls, and he was alone in the house. It was a warm afternoon, and he said he was going to get some lemonade, and would I like some before I went. I followed him into the kitchen, and he started as usual with his tickling and 'play fighting' up against the counter, and very quickly he was all over me." Brenda sat reliving the moment, in tears - that pivotal moment when her life changed forever.

"When I got home, I told my ma and daddy, but they just said I mustn't be making up stories like that - and it was Kevin just being a playful eejit, like he always was. 'He's a family man and wouldn't be doing anything like that, so stop your nonsense'," she dabbed at her eyes, "Well you know what happens - nature took its course and I started showing and mam kept me indoors with the shame of it. My da still accused me of making the story up, and was convinced it was my Michael had gotten me in this state last time he was home, and wouldn't believe me when I said we'd never done… that together - he even took to blaming me for my situation, for wearing my skirts too short.

"So, soon after, Mam got the priest in to talk to me, and it was him that promised me that I'd be cared for by the Sisters of Our Lady in a nursing home, until the baby was born, and that they could arrange for a good Catholic family to care for it. Well, that sounded OK, I supposed, and at least I could maybe pick up the pieces again with Michael, when it was over. He'd been away at a cousin's farm in west Cork, down past Bantry way, and I'd written to him to tell him my… situation. I'd not had a reply from him before I went off to Dublin - and, as I found out later, he was never even given my letter."

Brenda settled back in her chair, visibly drained from recounting it all again. Andy, who was sat next to her, held her arm, "I can't imagine how you found the strength to carry on, especially with the kind of 'care' it sounds like you were given."

She smiled at him and Gino, "well it was worth the pain when you two arrived, such beautiful boys with that shock of dark red hair - and the nuns were all over you. I had a very special few weeks, feeding and looking after yous both. And well, you know what happened next. I went into the nursery one morning, and you were both gone, the cots empty. Sister Bernadette had already put my few things together in a bag, and I was taken over to the Magdalene on Sean McDermott Street."

"Sinead said you were put to work scrubbing the floors?"

"Yes, so I was. There were quite a few of us in there - all beaten down, and we were quickly sucked down into the institution, given our tasks. Us new girls did the hardest jobs like the floors. It was the shame all us women had to live with, that the nuns drummed into us, made us just conform, God help us."

She recounted how the next few years went on, just as Sinead had described it. "It's so strange; it's like I'm telling a story about somebody else. I've never spoken about it before, apart from to Michael, he knew what I'd been through from the beginning, of course. He's been my rock all these years. But it's like I'm trying to just tell a story - and then it hits me that that was me. I was the one living through it all - those nuns were doing all that to me."

"So what happened to Kevin?"

"He just carried on from what I heard, Gino. I'd not stayed in touch with anyone at home. No doubt he carried on as before, but I've no idea as I'd lost all contact with everyone from home."

Andy asked her about the Irish government restitution he'd read about, and how the nuns and the church have not been held to account. She talked about the cases that Sinead had mentioned, and what a fight it was to get anywhere, "and those that win are only offered a token amount of money, nowhere near enough for all the hurt. Quite a few girls couldn't live with it and ended their own lives, so I've heard."

She was sad about the estrangement from her family, "My letters home were never answered, though I'd heard later on that our letters, which the nuns got us to write every week, were never sent to our families, so I suppose it's not surprising. I wasn't too surprised when I found out much later that my Ma had been writing to me, but gave up after a year or so when I'd not replied. It was an awful cruelty, it was.

"So, I'd not had any contact even years later after we were married. Eventually I heard from my sisters. Fionnula and Geraldine both sent me a card a few years later, after they'd heard about Sinead being born, with a bit of their news. And they only heard about that from Michael's sister back home." She took a drink of her tea, "Agh, it's gone cold - that's me gabbing on so much," she smiled.

"Later on, we did eventually visit my Mam, more out of duty - and I couldn't even look at Da, there was no love left there, and he only grudgingly acknowledged his own granddaughter, Sinead. I took my comfort in the love I had in my own family here. I never forgot yous two though - I lit a candle every birthday and

Christmas for each of yous, so I did. I'd sit in the pew, watching the two flames, wondering where you were and how you were both doing. Hoping for enlightenment maybe."

"That's almost poetic, Mam,"

"Yes indeed Andy - it was a comfort. Oh, and I so loved it when I heard that your own mothers both had the same thought, and lit a candle for me on each birthday… for me! …and with them not knowing each other as well. That thought had me in tears for days. It was so cruel that you were separated; what were the nuns thinking? They didn't say anything about it, just that they'd found a good catholic family who would love yous both... If only I'd known."

"I know, my own mom said she'd no idea we were twins, and would gladly have adopted both of us if she'd known. Same goes for Andy's mother. I'm real glad we found each other eventually - and you of course, Mam."

"Oh, dear God," she looked at the two of them and smiled, "He or someone up there must have been looking down on us all to make that happen. What'd be the odds on yous two, living in different countries, finding each other? Something put the idea of going to New York into Andy's head. I don't care now who or what it was, I'm just thankful it did."

"So are we both, Mam."

"Oh, Dear Lord, I could get used to hearing that being said by yous both," they all laughed. Sinead came back into the room, bringing sandwiches and cake for lunch, and a huge pot of tea, "I'm sorry Gino, I hadn't thought earlier. Do you drink tea?"

"Sure, I can get by with it - Andy here keeps making it for me." While they were eating, the two boys told them more about their other mothers, and Jeannette's recent visit to Long Island. Brenda told them that she was unsure about what their mothers might think of her, having been pregnant out of wedlock and then giving up two babies. Andy held her arm again, "That's not even a thought for either of them, their hearts went out to you when we told them after our first Zoom call with these two," he said, looking at Sinead and Niall."

"Too right, Andy. When we were all out at Mom's house last weekend, we spoke a lot about you. They both feel indebted to you, and so saddened by what you went through."

They both told Brenda more about their lives in London and New York, their groups of friends and how this last month or so had been such a massive change for them both.

A car pulled up outside later in the afternoon and Michael arrived back for tea. Brenda got up to meet him at the door and took him through into the kitchen.

Gino looked quizzically at Sinead, who nodded, "Mam wants to prepare Daddy for the new faces in here. She said she wanted to check what he remembered about the twins and you two coming over. He was clear as a bell the other day, when we were speaking about it all."

"So is it not too far advanced?"

"Not too bad Gino - though it varies from day to day. He should be good today, as he's been at the lunch club."

Another car arrived shortly after, and the other three sisters arrived, all carrying bags and storage boxes. "Ah here they are - and my word, it looks like there's enough food and cake there to feed an army!" Sinead cried, as she opened the door, and more quietly, "will yous all come in the front room, Mam's in the kitchen with our Daddy. Come in here and meet your brothers!"

"Hello, hello, hello!" rang out all round, Sinead did the introductions, "Aisling, Niamh, Maireadh - though you'll have forgotten who's who in 10 minutes," she laughed.

"Same here for these two lads," Niamh answered, "though from your hair I can tell you must be Andy - is that right?"

"Yeah, the relaxed look Niall called it"

Gino shot back, "I keep trying to get him to a decent barber - no luck yet," as they laughed.

"No, no, you keep it that way at least we can tell yous apart. And I see you've both got Niall's dimple," Aisling laughed. "But it's wonderful to finally meet yous both. As these two probably told you, we've all been agog with what's been coming out in the last few weeks."

"I can well believe it Aisling, I suppose it's been a massive change for all of us."

"It has indeed Andy. Oh, and did Sinead manage to tell you that I'd spent a couple of years working in London, at the Kings College Hospital? I went over after I left nursing college."

"No way, my mum was a midwife there as well - a while back of course."

"Sinead had mentioned that was where you grew up, living in Brixton. That's where I shared a flat with two other nurses, just off Coldharbour Lane."

"Just like my mum did when she first moved there. We had a bigger flat not far away after I was adopted. I'm thinking that we'd probably moved to Morden by the time you were there - and mum was probably working at the St. Helier by then. So near but so far!" They chatted a bit about places they both knew from their lives in South London, "so it sounds like we may have both gone to the Inferno's club at Clapham Common around the same time. Now there's a real coincidence!"

Aisling looked thoughtful, "Well, I suppose it's a good thing that we didn't meet each other there, with you turning out to be my brother and all!! Now, that could have been awkward, eh Sinead!"

"Ah Jaysus, I'd never even thought about any of that, with you not knowing you were both related. I do wonder if it has ever happened before. I'll bet it has somewhere. Now that would be another whole can of worms indeed. I guess it is less likely to happen nowadays, that people have a better record of their birth family."

"That sure is something to think about - I guess I was safe in New York, eh Sinead?"

"You were safe from us all, we're all firmly this side of the pond, Gino." They laughed, and conversation flowed, thinking about how couples would deal with the situation.

Just then, Mam came back in the living room with Michael, "sorry to leave yous all in here on your own," and a chorus of "Hi Daddy" rang round from the girls.

"Now Michael, you obviously know this bunch here - meet Andy there - and Gino."

"Well lads, your Mam here has been waiting a lot of years for you two to turn up. What on earth kept yous?" They all laughed, as Michael came over and sat with the two new twins,

"I'm not sure if you both know how much this means to Brenda - your Mam, with you two wanting to find her. She spent a lifetime thinking about yous, and living with the rejection from her own family, and the Church - and I know there was always that thought in the back of her mind, that you might have had the thought she'd rejected you, and just had you taken away. She'd have hated yous both thinking that about her."

"Absolutely not Michael - can I call you Michael?"

"My friends call me Mick - you can count me as a friend, for wanting to make my Brenda happy - well, for as long as my mind lasts anyway. You should know that I can forget things, and sometimes say something a bit odd."

"Thanks Mick, Sinead mentioned your diagnosis, so don't worry about us - and Andy's right, we both always knew we were adopted, and both our mothers told us that sometimes it's not the mother's decision to give a baby up for adoption."

"We'd no idea of the actual story though - what a life she - well you both have had. I know Gino will agree, I am proud to call you a friend, for the love and support you have given her."

Mick was visibly touched, and patted Andy and Gino on the shoulder.

"You OK Daddy?"

"Couldn't be better Sinead, couldn't be better. I've all you lot crowding out our house and making a mess, and now these two to cap it all," he replied smiling.

"Hey Daddy, did we tell you that Gino's mom gave him Michael as a middle name?"

"Yeah, she wanted to keep something Irish for where I came from - and would you believe Andy here is Andrew Patrick. Our mothers must have been on the same wavelength even back then without realising it."

Brenda went quiet, her eyes moistening again, "I'm just so shocked that the nuns had kept both your names - the ones I chose for you both," she wiped her eyes again, "I'd never told you what

I'd named them Michael, after you and my Granda. I just kept that as my own little secret - it just felt wrong, you know..." as she hugged her husband.

"Well, that's just grand, eh Brenda? Who'd have thought it? So, you boys have had the names Brenda gave you your whole life, and never knew it. We're just so blessed to have you here lads - and blessed that yous both have come back into her life."

Niamh and Maireadh burst back into the room together, "Now there's a pile of food laid out in the kitchen, with plates and cutlery and even serviettes (aren't we posh, eh!). We've not a table big enough, so you'll have to perch on your laps somewhere, anywhere - you boys are family now so that goes for you as well," she laughed.

As he ate, Andy was thinking what a wonderful way to cap off what was a life changing day for them all, and they shared more of their memories of their years growing up - in London and New York. Andy thought it was time to mention that their mothers were wanting to meet her, and turned to Brenda, "Mam, one thing I want to ask, did Sinead tell you that our mothers would love to come and meet you as well?"

"She did say something of it, yes," she answered, touching his arm - but almost shrinking back, "but I'm not sure what they would make of me - a simple Waterford girl."

"Well," Gino continued, "Like we said before, they both hold you in high regard - you know they are eternally grateful to you for... for us, and for all you've been through. I'm sure you'd all get along just fine."

Mam's thoughts

"Oh my, my, what a day this has been. My God, my God, how wonderful to have had those lovely twins back with me, even for just this day - along with all my other children.

"And how wonderful that my Michael was still of a mind to really know that these were the twins I'd had taken from me all those years ago. He is

still so angry with that Kevin Walsh - that kind of thing goes deep, it does. So I'm glad that the boys haven't taken a look from him though, so I am. I love that they've a bit of a look of Niall.

"This day there has been so much said and talked about, it's hard to take it all in. My head's bursting with all the things they told me about their lives. It's lovely to know they're both so artsy, like my own Da and our Sinead. And how about that, meeting up in New York after all that time, eh? I couldn't believe it when Sinead first told me. What a tale - what a tale.

"I want to tell the whole world that I've found my twin boys - but there's still that poison from the nuns in my head, I'm still hung up on the shame they drilled into me. But to hell with them - and that's where they all deserve to be.

"I love it, that Gino and Andy told me that their mothers both want to meet me - to say 'thank you' to me, that's what Gino said. That could be a lovely idea, though I must say I'm a little unsure in myself. How would I come across? With me getting pregnant so young - there's me at it again, with my Da in my head, blaming me for leading that Kevin on.

"Yes, I would like to meet them. I really want to thank them from the bottom of my heart, for all their hard work turning out two such wonderful boys."

Another New York Tuesday

It was another Manhattan Tuesday morning for Andy - yes Tuesday had become a special day for him… and Gino as well, since they first met up.

During his subway ride in to work, he replayed the events and conversations of the last weekend, turning over the details in his mind. Andy was more rushed than usual, wanting to get through a few admin tasks ahead of a conference call, so he grabbed a quick coffee on the way through Bryant Park heading to the office. Out of context completely, he found himself waiting at the crosswalk almost next to Michelle. He reached out and tapped her elbow, "hey, what are you doing in this part of town?"

"Oh, Andy! Great to see you - I was just thinking that you work somewhere round here. I've a meeting this morning a coupla streets away. And, hey - I get it now - what you meant when you talked about coming through this park in the mornings. It really is a little oasis of calm - well, as calm as Manhattan ever gets, I guess," she laughed, "but anyway, how was your trip to Ireland?"

"Listen, I'm in a dash to get to the studio - how about we meet up later if you have time? I can update you on our trip to 'the auld country'." he laughed.

"Sure Andy - I'll be clear around 11.45, if that works for you."

"Sure - early lunch? We can get something here in a cafe in the park - Porch maybe?"

"Sounds perfect Andy - I'll see you later on." and they had a quick hug and she crossed over. Andy got to the office and took the elevator, waving to Serena as he rushed into the studio, settling at his desk.

"Morning Denny! Hey, you'll never guess who I'm having lunch with."

"Go on then - Michelle Pfeiffer? Dakota Fanning?" they laughed,

"No, but you're close - it's our own Michelle - I just bumped into her on the street, on the way through the park. She's got a client meeting somewhere nearby this morning."

"Oh, interesting," Denny smiled, stroking his chin, "and this is…?"

"Hey - it's just lunch - that's all. She's already tried dating one twin - and Gino and I are so alike in a lot of ways - including being crap at relationships! So - it's lunch. I said I'd bring her up to date on what happened last weekend - the latest from the 'podcast'," he laughed.

"Ah OK, makes sense. She'll have to pin her ears back. That sounded like an amazing weekend from everything you told me yesterday. I'm sure that will all make for some interesting conversation dude!"

Andy broke off a bit earlier than he needed, so he could be sure of getting a table at Porch, which he knew was always pretty busy. He waved to Denny and Serena as he left. Arriving a little early had proved a useful strategy. As he sat and waited for Michelle, the tables were filling up. He waved to her as she came in.

"Hey - did you have a productive morning?" as they air kissed.

"Hiya, yes I got plenty done - how was your meeting - useful?" he asked.

"Very much so. It's an existing client relationship, so I am just pitching for a renovation of offices down in Chelsea, not far from the markets."

"Ah yes, I love it down there, just so different to midtown. Is it a big contract?"

"Fair size, and I've a good feeling we'll get the job - they just have to go through the motions of tendering, and I think they've more in the pipeline in the same building. Anyhow - that's not important. How was your trip to Dublin? What's the family like?"

"They're a really nice, grounded family - in spite of what Brenda has been through, it's quite remarkable really. We met Sinead and Niall of course, and their three sisters, so it was a real nice houseful. We heard a whole *lot* more from her, about her life and experiences. And it was an amazing emotional rollercoaster, Michelle, almost from the moment Sinead collected us from the airport."

"Oh wow, in what way?"

"Well, you were aware that Brenda was pregnant with us two, as a teenager - and that none of the rest of the family knew anything of her back story?"

"Yeah,"

"Brenda was 'taken advantage of' - well, raped in reality, by the church youth group leader - who was also a family friend, and…"

"Oh my God!!" Michelle gasped.

"…and of course she was not believed - they tried blaming her boyfriend - childhood sweetheart - but he was away working on a cousin's farm that year." Andy recounted the details of her then being sent away to the nuns' mother and baby home in Dublin - and then the horrors of the Magdalene laundry system. They broke off for a moment as the waiter came over, to order their food.

"There was also the glimmer of christian charity from the one nun, who helped her get out and organised a job for her on the outside. And then she told me how her sweetheart from home, Michael, had moved to Dublin with work, in the hope of finding her. He knew she'd been sent there, but no idea where. He had done some searching but had nothing to go on.

But, against all the odds, some time later, he was sent into Dublin to pick up some printed stationery from the very stationers she was working in! You couldn't write it - but it happened. They got back together again - Brenda shared her horror story with him, but that didn't matter to Michael. He just wanted her for herself. Very romantic, eh?"

"So Michael was her knight in shining armour! Wow, what a tale,"

"Yes he was - and they were married not long after, and had Sinead and Niall, who we've been talking to - and then the three other girls. And underneath the awfulness of her story, I could feel that she was strong and… and resilient - which is mostly from her, then underpinned by her husband. We met them all while we were over there. Michael - Mick came along later and was so grateful that we'd come looking for her."

"…and if we hadn't just randomly met this morning, when would I have heard all this news, eh?" she asked.

He nodded, "Yeah, good point. We need another 'lost twins podcast' episode! Hey, it's hard enough for us two to keep up with all this. If you wrote it in a book you'd not believe it!" he laughed. "Anyway, that's you pretty much up to date now, apart from the possibility of Angie and my Mum both going to visit our Mam in Dublin, which she is thinking about as far as I know. Anyway, I also thought you'd be able to tell me a bit more about yourself today as well. When Max is around, he takes all the oxygen almost," they both laughed.

Michelle told Andy more about her growing up in New Jersey and college at Baruch. That led to a career in real estate. First lettings, then commercial and then dealing with negotiations and contracts in the same kind of business as Max, commercial office fit outs. They had worked together a couple of jobs back, which is where they first met.

She then went a little more into her own mom's search for grandma's first child - and how it would probably have to wait until she took the step of doing a DNA search to get any connection, "that's why what you guys are going through is so fascinating."

They moved on as Andy asked more about Gino and Max's friendship - mentioning that he'd heard that she and Gino had dated a while back. "Yeah - we did, but I'm sure Gino told you that we were too much like old friends. It felt - not quite…"

"You mean, not like going on a date with a stranger then, maybe?"

"Yeah - I think that may be what it is."

"I was thinking that you being friends would make it more… more comfortable, maybe."

"Yeah - comfortable, exactly right. But maybe too comfortable to take it seriously. Like old bedroom slippers," she laughed. Michelle looked back up, "I hear that you and he are similar in that as well as so much else - not finding the right person to connect with?"

"Too right - you're not wrong there. I was engaged for a while, when I lived in London, after that, well, I thought a clean break would be good for me - then I saw this job come up. I've been on a few dates since coming over here - but nothing serious that I could have seen go beyond, you know…"

"I know what you mean - too well." Changing tack, she asks, "so, I was talking to your mom when she was here, she said you were a bit of a jazz lover. That right?"

"I am a bit - I think I caught the bug from my dad. I'm still into the music I grew up with - Stone Roses, Oasis, Ocean Colour Scene but I love Dad's old stuff too, you know, the Caribbean sounds. And I just love the sounds of jazz guitar - it's that rich mellow sound. Not so much the old gypsy Django Reinahrdt style, I'm more into players like George Benson, Jim Hall - like Mum was probably telling you when you met."

"Me too, actually. Funnily enough, I'm going to see a really great New York guitarist, Allan Bezama at the Django club tomorrow if you fancy it Andy - and if you're free of course."

"I don't think I know him - though I might have heard him on the Pure Jazz station of course. And I've not been to the Django either, though I know of the club and keep meaning to make the effort. Whereabouts is it - is it in Tribeca area?"

"Yeah, way down below Canal Street, in the basement of the Roxy Hotel, near Tribeca Park. Allan's a real up and coming talent, so he's still playing the smaller clubs. I'm thinking you'll like him."

"OK sure, that sounds good and make a change, and it beats another evening talking football in the local bar. And, as I said, I've never been to Django's, so yes, great idea. What time is it?"

"Starts pretty early - 6.30 - and we can get some food there if that works. They do all sorts from small plates up."

Back in the studio later on, Andy tells Denny how Michelle took in the news from their trip to see Sinead and Brenda, "yeah, she felt a bit left out of the loop - I'm assuming Gino will have updated Max already; I'll ping him a WhatsApp and ask anyway."

"Sounds a solid idea bud, that is quite a big story to take in. So… when are you seeing Michelle again?" he smiled.

"Er… actually, tomorrow evening," Andy admitted.

"Ha, ha," Denny laughed, "now, that sounds very much like a date to me, man!"

"Nah…" Andy thought about it, "though I suppose it could look that way. But honestly, we were talking about jazz - and she's going to a gig tomorrow, and just asked if I'd like to go along."

"THAT, my dear Andy - that sounds like you've been dated, to me. No question!" he laughed, "you've been hooked."

"Don't be daft - I'm sure it will be just a couple of friends enjoying a jazz gig," said Andy, a little bashfully. He'd not really twigged it. But Denny was right, it did certainly feel like he's been asked out on a date - 'eh well, I'll just have to see how it goes I guess' he thought to himself.

It was certainly an interesting thought and he turned it over in his mind, how he should approach it during the afternoon's work. Michelle was a very attractive woman, and they seemed to get on really well over lunch... Gino had already said that there was nothing there between them, but could there be some kind of sibling rivalry rear its head - though maybe their own relationship was a bit new for any of that. Who knows?

He tried to put it out of mind for the rest of the day, as he buried himself in the packaging designs, and merchandising style sheets for a new flavour of potato chips. More cutting edge creativity - but he knew the commercial value of the work to the client, was a world away from what he'd have been working on in London. So of course were the billings - and thankfully, given the cost of living in the US, so was his salary!

$$\text{—— } 26 \text{ ——}$$

A Date?

On the journey home to Queens, Andy was thinking he should call Gino, just to talk through the Michelle thing - 'date' - whatever - and get a feel for how the land lay with him and Michelle. Of course, he'd already told Andy that there wasn't anything there between them, and Michelle told him the same earlier. Though it could be denial from either side - who knows. The last thing he wanted to do was cause any awkwardness - his relationship with Gino was too important for that.

He'd told himself in all honesty, he'd not seen the 'date' the next evening as being - a date. Life had just become a lot more complicated; he was used to having a brother, though there was little rivalry in that way, as they had very different circles of friends. Gino hadn't had that experience to fall back on, though the fact that he and Max had dated Michelle at different times may have roused a similar feeling of rivalry for them, maybe.

And - of course - there is a weird possibility that if Michelle still has a thing for Gino - even unconsciously, she could view him as a kind of stand in for Gino. 'Bugger' he thought, yeah - it makes sense, he needed to talk to Gino.

By the time he'd wrestled with all that, he was nearly back in Woodside - he rang Gino to see if he was free for a chat over a beer later. That would be the best way to talk it through - after all Gino was fast becoming his best friend, as well as being his twin.

They met in the Irish Whiskey Bar near Astoria, which Gino thought sounded appropriate. They both just had a beer though. There was a singer guitar duo playing a live set in the place. "I've not come across this place before, Gino. Quite a cool vibe."

"I've not been in many times - just seemed appropriate," Gino smiled, "anyway, what's happening?"

"I bumped into Michelle this morning on the way into work, near Bryant Park, completely out of context. She suggested going for lunch so I could update her on last weekend. She was so shocked by what I told her of Mam's ordeal with the nuns and the Magdalene laundry."

Andy then set about explaining the scenario of her suggesting he join her at a jazz club down in Tribeca the next evening. And, he talked him through the mental gymnastics he had had on the train back home earlier, "so what's your view? Is it a date - and I'm too dense to realise - or is it just two friends enjoying some music?"

"Ha ha, I see where you're coming from, man. And no, I've no idea if she still hung up on me - it doesn't seem that way to me. She's just so… natural. One of the guys."

"I know, so I've no idea how to deal with it - I was fine with being two friends who like music, 'til Denny put that idea into my head."

"Got it. But I know she loves jazz and is often out to gigs on her own. And I heard her talking with your mom in Dillon's about jazz music - there was a track they both liked that was playing. Maybe it is as simple as that. Anyways, I've not got a problem if she has the hots for you. If it turns out she hasn't, then she's still a good friend and you've had a fun evening out."

"I suppose that's the way to think about it, you're right. But look at it from her side. How weird would it be - if this is how it goes - to date an ex's twin brother?"

"That could be a bit… awkward maybe… comparing us two," they both laughed at the thought.

"But… I suppose we might look almost the same but we're different people. It could be more awkward for her, you know, in… 'intimate situations'… getting mixed up? But - that's way ahead, maybe I'm overthinking it all. We are just going to listen to a great guitarist play some music; nothing more. Simple," they laughed again.

"But hey, let me know how it goes bro!"

— 27 —

A Date

Andy left the office a little earlier than usual that Wednesday afternoon, to take the subway down to Canal Street, and he came out on the street close to the Tribeca park, and luckily just about on time to meet Michelle outside the Roxy Hotel, thoughts of his discussions with Denny and Gino still fresh in his mind. 'Just take it as it comes', he told himself, 'we're just pals'.

"Hey Andy," she waved, "bang on time - great to see you. Thanks for coming along - it's going to be a fun evening," as they air kissed, and walked round to the entrance of Django's jazz club.

"What an amazing building Michelle. A real Art Deco masterpiece, I can't believe I've not seen it before."

"It certainly is. It's an original bit of the Tribeca scene. There's usually good music, so well worth the half-hour subway trip to visit. I've made a res - this guy can pack the place out, so I didn't want to just show up last minute."

They followed the signs down to the cellar venue, remembering that someone once said that the best jazz was always found below street level. They emerged into the wonderful vaulted space and were shown to their table, not too far from the stage, where the sound guy was checking mikes and cables.

They talked for a while, as he told Michelle about his evening out with Gino 'on the town' in Dublin, visiting Sinead's gallery, brother Niall who shared their dimpled chin - and the other sisters, and the lovely chaos of eating with the family.

"But more important, how was Brenda with the two of you? it must have felt like a weird situation for all of you?"

"I know - but it actually felt strangely natural. Of course, we've spoken to Sinead and Niall a fair bit on Zoom anyway. So we knew each other really, and conversation just flowed - carried on really from before. When we met, she was most struck by how we looked taller than on screen."

"Ha ha, ain't that the way. I had a new colleague who worked remote through Covid lockdown - and I just didn't recognise him when I met him in the office later. He's six foot nine!" she laughed, "and what was Brenda like?"

"She was so lovely - and we could tell she loved having us two there - and all her family." As their server came past, they ordered a couple of cocktails to start the evening off, as Allan Bezama and his trio took to the stage. Michelle was right, the place did get packed out, with more people still arriving. Andy caught himself thinking what a great place to bring a date - bringing Denny's jibe to mind again. Though usually he'd have taken a date for a dinner, or a few drinks and maybe on for food if they clicked.

This was different, he told himself. This was two friends sharing a love of music, and this guy's guitar style did not disappoint, and he turned and smiled at Michelle as they clapped after the first piece. "You were right, really cool venue and great guitarist."

In gaps between the pieces, Andy told Michelle more about the three sisters, and the coincidence of Aisling having worked - and gone clubbing - near where he lived in London. "We had an interesting chat about what might have happened if we'd both met up randomly."

"Oh man, that could have been awkward, if you'd... you know..."

"That's exactly what we all said," Andy laughed, "and it was great meeting Brenda's husband Michael as well, and hearing his side of her story. He told us to call him Mick, as that's what his friends call him. He gave us a proper welcome into the family." Andy gave her the full picture of their weekend over in Dublin, while they shared a few of the small plates from the menu.

The evening had more than lived up to expectations, as they finished their drinks and came back up to street level, past the elegant Roxy entrance into the cool evening air. The street was calmer in the cool of the early summer evening, as they walked back towards the Canal Street subway stations.

"What a great evening Michelle, thanks so much for suggesting it. Makes a real change from watching football… soccer, over a few beers."

"Hey, it was my pleasure, it's nice to have the company - and to get to know you a bit better of course. Usually I'm on my own, as not many other friends are as into jazz as much as me. It's good to find another jazz geek." she laughed. As they reached the subway, she told him, "I'm taking the A train - I know that sounds a little corny for a jazz lover!" she laughed again, "takes me home to my place in Harlem."

"Makes me wonder - is that what that song's about - going up to Harlem? I'm going to have to find out if it is," he laughed, "OK, I'm on the W train - a bit less poetic, and then a change as well, I think."

"Oh, of course, you live in Queens, like Gino, don't you," as she leaned into him and they hugged, "and it's been a lovely evening Andy - and thanks so much for dinner and for your company again," and waved, as they went their separate ways.

As he waited on the platform, Andy turned the evening over in his mind, mulling over what she'd said, and thinking that it couldn't have gone much better really. They were easy and natural with each other - really comfortable body language. Maybe it was because unlike an actual 'date' date, there were no expectations. As a friendship, it was really… comfortable, that's what it was. And one to build on - whatever direction it took from here on.

Brenda & her twins

Next morning at breakfast, Andy saw a WhatsApp from Sinead. She asked if he and Gino would like to have a Zoom call with her mam.

As he was reading it, Gino pinged back to say 'sure that would be great, when are you thinking.' Sinead suggested 'evening our time, will make it mid afternoon for you. Would that work?' and then saw the three dots as Gino came back, 'are you thinking Saturday?' And Sinead answered with a thumbs up. Andy responded, 'Sounds good Sinead - we can be separate or it may be better if I go over to Gino's - so we're on the same screen for her' and Gino added 'great idea - I'll do lunch'.

Gino called him straight afterwards, "I'll be out first thing Saturday but do you want to get here sometime after 11?"

"Sure, that sounds great."

Andy walked the mile or so over to Gino's place in Astoria on the Saturday morning, arriving just as Gino's cab pulled up at his apartment and they chatted about the week, as they put lunch together - tuna salad with olives. Andy told Gino all about his evening with Michelle, and how really nice it was. "I'm still no clearer if there's anything there, in that way. But, just take everything as it comes, I suppose."

After lunch Gino made coffee and they set up the laptop, ready for the afternoon call with Brenda. Sinead had helped her to set up their call on her own laptop. Their faces appeared and all waved.

"Well hello you two, how lovely to see yous again. I can't believe you're all those miles away."

"Hello to you two as well, how're you both doing?"

"We're all fine here and still talking all about your trip over here. It was so lovely to have you here with me and with the rest of my brood as well." Brenda wanted to hear more about their lives and work, and to get to know them a bit better. She asked them about their earliest memories, and Andy and Gino talk about their younger days, school and growing up and their parents' lives, and Brenda took it all in, as Niall again arrived a bit behind, bringing cups of tea for them all.

Gino wanted to know more about Brenda's 'escape', "So how did you deal with the switch from being stuck in the laundry to working on the outside? That must have been such a massive change to get your head around."

"Sure, it was. Took me from not even being my own person, to… to… freedom I'd suppose you'd call it. The hardest part was trying to break away from that numbing sense of shame - that we all felt in there, you know - but none of us at the laundry ever talked about. It just dragged you down it did.

"There were some brief happy moments but they were few and far between. It's odd, but I've never made contact with any of the other girls from there. I did see one of them, Siobhan along O'Connell Street once, but we just looked through each other. Thinking about it, I suppose we couldn't even bring ourselves to acknowledge what had happened to either of us.

"When I got the office job, you're right, I found it so hard to adjust. I didn't know how to talk to folk - or to trust anyone. Though on my first day in the job, I was met with a kindness I'd not encountered for ages. When the front shop closed up for lunch time, Eileen asked what I'd brought to eat - of course I had nothing, and no money to buy anything with. I felt awful and just said I'd forgotten to bring anything. So she shared her sandwiches with me; I almost wept with the kindness.

"I'm sure she knew what had happened to me and probably where I'd actually come from, though no-one said anything; I was told to say that I'd come up from Waterford for the job. Anyways, later on that first day, when she asked where I was living, I'm sure that she must have guessed something, as she said her mam had a spare room that she was sure I could use til I got on my feet."

"So do you think that she really knew where you'd come from?"

"I'd no way of knowing, Andy… and I certainly wasn't going to ask if she knew. Maybe it was the raggedy way I was dressed? Looking back even weeks later, I realised how awful my clothes were - worn out and faded with a hole in my shoe. I'm sure neither Eileen nor her mam believed my story that I'd lost my suitcase on the train, when I think about it. She let me borrow a few things of hers that week. It was the first Christian kindness I'd had in so many years. I didn't know where to place myself. But Eileen and her mam were kindness itself, so they were."

"That must have been a huge leap for you - going back to almost a normal life?"

"Oh yes indeed, I can't tell yous how much - I'd forgotten what 'normal life' was even.. During that first week it was really hard. Eileen's mam had asked if I'd like to stay, and how much could I afford for the housekeeping, and I had no idea at all. So, I got paid on the Friday, £45 - it was Irish Punts in those days of course - which was a king's ransom to me; we agreed on £20 for housekeeping - and actually had some money left of my own. First time I'd ever had my own money. Now that was a new experience for me - I had to buy a purse to put it in," she laughed, "and it meant I could buy some clothes of my own and a lipstick, they were the first things I had owned since I left home."

"Oh, and her mam cooked us such lovely dinners, and a packed lunch for work, just like at home and they made me so so welcome. It was hard to talk about myself, and I got to be quite skillful at steering conversation away from me, and my past to nicer things. Even a few years later, Eileen and I would both skirt around talking about that time.

"So, you're right to ask - it really was not easy adapting to such a change, and in my mind I kept going from homesickness for my old family, to anger that Mam and Da would put me through all that awfulness - and back again. But I wasn't going to go home.

"Then later on, Eileen's mam helped me to find proper digs of my own, with my own bathroom would you believe, in a nice house in Drumcondra, staying with a middle aged couple. So I was starting to get on my feet a bit."

"That would have been such a difference, from where you'd been before."

"Oh yes Andy, so it was. It was like living in a palace - even compared to our house back home. And then… Michael walked back into my life - coming into the front shop at Doyle's stationers, to collect some printed Invoices and bill heads for his work. I couldn't believe my eyes, my heart leapt in my chest and I froze - just froze.

"I didn't know what to do with myself. I tried to keep my head down and hide away, I knew that he'd know what had happened to me, and I had no idea what he thought of me now. All that damned shame, knocked into me by the nuns. But I heard his voice when he was talking to Eileen on the counter - and I can hear it still in my head - 'can I speak to Brenda Kelly please?' Well, he'd seen me and I didn't know where to put myself - I nearly fell through the floor," Brenda drifted off remembering it all… then carried on, "He was so much taller now, and handsome. My Michael! I couldn't believe it, I couldn't.

"Well, I went up and spoke with him and I must have been so red faced. He smiled and didn't say a thing about… you know, and he just put me at ease, asking how I was and everything. And we arranged to meet up in town after work that day. Eileen was so excited for me and asked a bit about him - I told the story of us being childhood sweethearts, but missing out those few years in the middle of course.

"He'd come up to Dublin and worked in a farm machinery place at that time, on the outskirts. He said he'd take the bus back into the City and perhaps we can go somewhere for our tea. I waited for him on O'Connell Street, and I saw him come round the corner, with such a confident stride, walking towards me and smiling… and we went along to The Kylemore Cafe and had Egg and Chips. My first proper date - ever! And we talked and talked. He told me about working on his cousin's farm, then getting a job in the local agricultural engineers firm, and then how he'd got the job in Dublin and why.

"I can tell you I was so choked up that he'd actually done all that… just to find me again. He'd guessed at what had happened to me anyway from the evasive answers from my Ma," she paused, then snapped back to being herself, "and well, yous both know the rest of the story."

"And this old story's still going on," Sinead added. "As I said when we spoke before, Mam's had none of this 'redress' the government has been trumpeting, same as so many of the others all over the country."

Andy nodded, "Yes, I read about Mary Cavan… Cavnar, was it?"

"Ah yes, the Mary Cavner court case,"

"It sounds like she really had to fight to get included in the scheme."

"Absolutely and fight she did - it took an age to get taken up and then took the case to the Ombudsman. The poor little thing, at just 11 years old, when her Da had died was carted off to the Industrial in Cork - and from then she spent years in slave labour for those damned nuns. Sorry Mammy, but I despise one and all of them. Eventually she got a payment - nowhere near enough to compensate for a lost life really. But - she got justice and it was that which drove her."

They talked over the issues of redress and whether it's worth chasing up. Brenda said that with Michael being the way he was, she wasn't minded to do all that. She was more than happy now that she had her expanded family. "I think you've picked up on how thrilled I am that you came looking for me - and coming over to visit. It's been such a joy to see you both and how you turned out."

"We'll be over again sometime soon I'm sure. I was saying as much to Gino. And you know that our mothers would love to come and visit you as well - but only if you want them to."

"…yeah, did we tell you, Jeannette had talked it through with my Mom when she was over here in New York - and get this, the idea came to her in a New York Irish pub!"

They all laughed, and Brenda said she would feel honoured to meet their mothers, so she could thank them for turning her babies into two such lovely chaps like yourselves.

After the call with Brenda, the boys reported back to their mothers, to let them know that Brenda would love to meet them. So it was just a matter of organising it - Gino suggested that the two of them should both fly across with Angie - but to let the three mothers meet up together first. Then see how it goes, or ask Sinead to organise somewhere to all go for dinner.

So the plan was hatched.

—— **29** ——

Tuesday in Manhattan

Another Tuesday. Andy sat there by the coffee stand thinking through how his life had changed in the six short weeks since Max had called to him, here in Bryant Park. He sat and watched as some of the usual faces passed, the runners cooling down, and all those others in conversation with friends or lovers.

That brief limbo he'd come to love, between the commute in and heading to the office. It was a time to think through what he wanted to achieve today - and again to mull over his 'date' the week before with Michelle at the Django - while taking in the morning air, still feeling a bit like late spring, though blossoming into a fresh early summer.

He also thought through how the next trip might go. He'd spoken with his mum the previous evening, and she said she'd go with whatever day works for him and Gino and Sinead and the family too. He'd call Gino later to go over the details.

He drank in the morning cool, sitting under the trees and sipping his Macchiato - before rousing himself to set off towards Madison and the office.

Gino called just before 9 to let him know Angie was excited, and that he'd message Sinead to arrange a call to arrange the trip for their mothers meeting up. She came back on WhatsApp and they arranged to do a Zoom over lunch from their offices with her as she'd be home by then.

The three of them appeared on the screen, and they said their hellos. Gino aired his suggestion for the meeting, "so we're thinking that we'll fly over with my mom on Friday, and let our three moms have some together to get to know each other properly."

"That sounds a good idea Gino, I think that would be a great way for them to meet."

"Then we thought we could join them either later for dinner - or the following day if that would be better. I think you'll have to judge how it goes - I know how both our mothers can talk - it may take a while!"

"And as you know, the same for our mam. Oh, and you know what has just struck me lads? It's so lovely that you're calling these three as mam, mom and mum. It makes so much sense, I can tell who's who!" she laughed.

"Ha ha, I'd not really thought about that - but it seems maybe a habit we've both slipped into."

"Oh and Sinead, Andy said that Jeannette was thinking that she and my 'mom' could have a quick Zoom call with your mam before actually meeting, if that would work for her - just an ice-breaker really so they'd all feel more comfortable when meeting up."

"That sounds a grand idea, Gino. Mam is getting used to all this technology now. She was asking if she could have an iPad for her birthday, so she did. Would you believe it?"

"Hey, great idea. She must want to keep an eye on us two!"

"That's sounds like you've got her number there Gino."

"On the timing, we've been thinking about coming over soon - so why not this week? Gino and I can both move some stuff around, and we all fly over on Friday so they can meet on Saturday. Maybe the mams can have a Zoom call together over the next day or so."

"Why not indeed Andy. No point in hanging around, I know Mam was excited at the idea, though as you know she feels more than a little unease about being judged for her early life."

"From what you and she have said, working through all that baggage dumped on her by the nuns will take some time. Especially having had to keep it a secret all these years."

"You're not wrong there Gino, to be sure."

Sinead messaged back under an hour later, to let them know that Mammy would love to see their mothers on a call - and can't wait to see them both again at the weekend. Gino did the bookings - the Beaumont Hotel again close to Mam's house - and flights again with Aer Lingus.

Andy booked his mum's flight from Gatwick and arranged with Leon to help her with the Zoom call - and to drive her to the airport on Saturday morning, to tie in with their overnight from JFK.

In honour of their very short held tradition, the team of friends met up that Tuesday evening again in Dillon's. "Can you believe it…" Michelle asked, "that it was only six weeks ago that you two met up here?"

"Sure has been some roller coaster ride."

"…and I keep having to remind myself that this has all actually happened. It's really been like following that podcast you talked about - and I'm there as a central character."

"'The official 'Lost Twins Podcast' eh Andy," Max laughed, "so when is that going live? Thought you were going to record something."

"I'd not really thought about us two being a 'story' and being newsworthy, though the check in girl at the airport thought it would make a good TV show, once she'd dealt with our confusing passports."

"Too right man. That was so funny."

"Sinead also told us that someone from the Herald newspaper in Dublin had contacted her. It seems that news about us is getting around anyway."

"Oh wow, Andy! Hey and are you kidding? This is one hell of a story, with all that's happened, in just six weeks, as Michelle said. I can just see you two on TV - NY1 or even 60 Minutes over here. It would make great TV."

Discussion turned to the trip the coming weekend and how Mam was feeling about meeting up with the two women who had adopted her babies. Andy shared what Brenda had said, wondering how they would view her, a simple Waterford girl, "and the saddest thing really is underlying all of that, she still lives with these mental scars of the shame drummed into her by those nuns. Even the way she holds herself sometimes - it almost feels… apologetic almost,"

"You're so right man. That's the feeling I get - but I'd not put into words as well as that."

"It sounds as though for all three of your mothers this is going to be quite some meet up." Michelle had summed it up pretty succinctly, and their evening moved to ordinary things on work and homes and other friends. For the twins, underlying all the gentle chat was the fact that their mothers were about to meet - to complete a fractured circle.

The group broke up as they headed for their subway rides home. Andy turned over everything from the evening as he waited on the platform for the subway. He felt his phone vibrate, and saw there was a message - from Michelle. 'Hey Jazz buddie. Have you ever been to Bill's place in Harlem? It's only on Fri and Sat nights - would be good to go together.'

OK, he thought… This is interesting - after all they'd been talking in Dillons all evening and she'd never mentioned it. He was thinking that hearing her say it, would give more clues than a simple text. He decided to call her as the cell signal was looking OK, "Hey Michelle. What's this about?"

"Oh, hi. Yeah, I was on my way back just now and it just came into my mind to wonder if you'd been up to any of the Harlem clubs. I was thinking Bill's as it's as real as it gets in a basement speakeasy. No frills - not even a bar, so it's a bring your own booze kinda joint."

"No, I've not - that sounds pretty cool. I'd love to go - when are you thinking?"

"Well Bill's only opens on Friday and Saturdays as I said. So perhaps next week after you're back from Dublin?"

"That sounds really cool actually. Should we eat first or after?"

"We'll need to book at Bill's - they do two shows a night, 7 or 9.30. I was thinking we could maybe go for a drink before the early show, then eat after. The Shrine Bar is just around the corner and serves til 10 and there's live music playing there most evenings. Should be fun."

"Well that sounds like... a date, I suppose!" laughed Andy, "Shall we make it the Saturday?"

"Perfect - I'll book the tickets to make sure we get in - it's just tiny - a real in your face experience!"

The train rattled into the station, looking almost empty. He sat and turned over his call with Michelle and wondered what had just happened. She certainly sounded excited at the idea of them going to Bill's.

He asked himself whether hearing it all, rather than a text, had made it any clearer for him, "Have I really been asked on a date? Or are we just 'Jazz buddies'. See where the evening takes us I guess." It could also be that perhaps she really is just working it out for herself as well, to see where it leads maybe. He left the subway smiling and wondering what the next steps would be.

30

Next steps

He'd shared the Michelle update with Denny during the next morning, "I hope you don't think I'm barging in there. I know you quite liked her."

"Hey, that's no problem, man. It sounds like you two get along - you're 'jazz buddies', eh? I get it. And it's another date - a proper one this time?"

"I've not worked that out yet - and I'm guessing neither has she. All we can do is play it by ear and see where it leads."

Over lunch, Andy got a call from Gino, "Hey bro, you remember Crissy?"

"Sure, you said you'd got on pretty well. Why - has she been in touch?"

"Oh yeah. She messaged me last night. Something like - no let me read it out: 'OK, I chose the restaurant last time. Your choice next and how about mid next week some time? You can bring me up to date with all your family stuff'."

"That there sounds promising."

"I must have made the right impression - and I said it felt like we had some kind of connection. She must have thought so too. I guess a girl can only wait so long for that second date."

"I like it that she's taken the initiative - it does sound like she wants it to go somewhere. Funnily enough, I had a message last night, on the subway home from Dillon's - from Michelle."

"Really. We'd only just seen her. What did she want?"

"Sounds like she's after a return fixture. She asked if her 'Jazz buddy' fancied a trip to a proper Harlem speakeasy - Bill's place. Do you know it?"

"No - I think I've heard Michelle talk about it. I think it's a famous sax player's own club or something."

"Yeah, it sounds like that from what she was saying. A 'bring your own booze' type place."

"This sounds like you've been dated, for real. What are you thinking about it?"

"I was thinking about it on the way this morning. I guess all I can do is play it by ear - and look for the signals - if I can remember them!" he laughed, "we're going for a drink first then the 7 o'clock show and eating after."

"That should give plenty of opportunity to read those signals, bro. And don't forget it's her home turf - she lives up in Harlem. Hey, that could make it a bit spicy!"

"I'd not put that fact into the mix. Oh jeez - does that make it a bit more…" he thought out loud, "hey, who knows Gino. It could just be a place she likes going."

"Oh yeah, yeah, I'm sure," Gino laughed, "but like you say, play it by ear."

They ended their conversation by going over the details for the flight to Dublin, just two days later, "so you're going to collect your mom on Friday morning, and we'll meet at JFK just before 3?"

"Yeah bro. This should be some trip. See you then."

During that afternoon, the thought of the 'next date', and what kind of 'date' it would turn into with Michelle, kept coming round in his mind. He was coming round to thinking about how their relationship would move along from being buddies - to something more involved. He got the feeling they could be good together.

And there was Gino too, going on a second date with Crissy. Had discovering their identical twin really changed them both so much? Perhaps that 'something missing' which he'd read about, had now had some kind of resolution, though he couldn't feel what, if anything, was different in him. He'd have to talk it through with Gino on the plane to Dublin, and get his take on it all.

Coupled to all of that of course, were thoughts of the three mothers meeting up over the coming weekend. A lot had happened in just these last few weeks - life had started to get interesting and he could think about more than the next design job or Chelsea match. Yes, life had started to get interesting.

31

The three mothers

Today is the day that Jeannette and Angie fly in to Dublin to actually meet Brenda, their sons' birth mother. Each of the mothers has her own thoughts on how this might go as you'd expect. Unusually for Dublin it's not raining - or even looking like it's thinking about it.

Angie, Gino and Andy were first to set off last night for the overnight on Aer Lingus, which is due to arrive at a similar time to Jeannette's from London. Sinead has borrowed Niall's seven seater to collect them at the airport - and she'll be meeting Jeannette off her flight first, so they can wait in the café she spotted in the arrivals hall for the flight from New York to come in.

Mom's thoughts

"This will have been the longest seven hours I've ever spent on a plane and shame we didn't get to sit together with the boys though I guess that may be useful, as hopefully I'll get a few hours sleep on the way; not easy in these seats.

"I really am the luckiest mother of a wonderful son. How absolutely amazing for him to have found his twin brother at this time in their lives. And I'm so thrilled that they started that search and found Brenda and her family too. It seems to have been a real whirlwind of a journey - ending up with me on a plane to Europe again!

"It will be lovely meeting Jeannette again too. We do seem to get along and I'm so glad she enjoyed her stay with me. What fun we had cooking together, learning each others' recipes. My, I'm going to have to try those

fresh ideas like that Barbados fish with cornmeal and okra. So simple and so delicious.

"And what fun it was to do all the sights as well. I've not really done any of that for years, and not at all since Joe passed. Coney Island hasn't changed a bit - well, a little bit. It's a little faded around the edges - but maybe that's the memory playing on it all.

"I can't help wondering how Brenda will be. It was lovely to have that video call with her and I think I can imagine some of what's running through her mind. We're the women that took her children - she sure didn't say as much but would she, deep down, resent all the time we had with them as babies, and going through school and everything?

"Perhaps that's just me overthinking it all, as she seemed pretty friendly on the call the other day and Gino didn't think so either; he'd said she was so happy - 'glowing' was the word Andy used.

"Anyways, that in-flight meal wasn't too awful I guess and it looks like the lights are going down now. I think I'll try and get some sleep - well at least rest my eyes - my mind's buzzing too much."

Turning off the M23 motorway which had taken them south from London, on to the spur for Gatwick airport, Leon following the signs for departures, turns and smiles at his mum, who's off to meet Angie again and then Brenda - the "mothers' summit meeting" as he'd joked earlier. They drive into the drop off zone, which, like so many now charges just to drop someone off. "What a pain that is!"

Offloading her bags, he gives his mum a kiss. Waving, she walks slowly into the departures, to go through all the rigmarole of security and all that. Turning, she waves again as she walks on through the doors.

Mum's thoughts

"I can't wait to see dear Angie again. It was such a wonderful time staying with her at her place on Long Island. I was just imagining her last night, tuking that drive to JFK airport for her flight over.

"What a wonderful and exciting time we had in New York, seeing the sights. We didn't really do much of that last time I went over to see Andrew. Coney Island really was like a huge Southend with all the candy floss and ice cream. It was lovely seeing all those other sights as well and the Guggenheim - smaller than I expected and the Met - bigger than I expected.

"Oh. and meeting all their friends in that Irish pub was such a super evening. Not my usual choice of pub I'll admit, with all that football and music going on - but it was so… kind of New York in itself. Max is such a hoot - and we've all got him to thank for starting all this off.

"I am so blessed with my two boys - and I think they feel closer together than ever before now, after that time in New York. Maybe it's just things dropped into place for them - getting to know each other again, out of context almost. It was lovely seeing them talking properly. It's been nice how Joseph got drawn into this whole thing as well. It was a bit like old times with him coming to Morden for lunch with Leon - he was almost as excited hearing all Andrew's news and about our trip to Long Island. Yes, he's been a good friend to me of late.

"So, all this thinking about myself - and despite talking with her this week on the ipad, I can't really imagine how Brenda must be feeling at this moment. I'm sooo glad that the boys' trip to Dublin went so well and she got to meet her babies again properly."

Driving north on the M1, Sinead heads out to the airport to meet Jeannette, then Angie and the boys. Everything is organised so they'll all be arriving not too far apart - Jeannette's flight from London first, then the lads and Angie's overnight flight from New York.

They're booked into the same hotel, the Beaumont, that the twins stayed in last time, so they'll be nearby and they can play the day by ear. Niall has a table booked in the hotel restaurant for the evening, in case they all want to go for dinner together later on.

Sinead had suggested to Gino that maybe their mothers would like to see some of Dublin while they're over, so she's pencilled in some ideas of places to go.

On the way to the airport, she thinks to herself, '*I do wonder how Mam will be, meeting the two other mothers - despite their on-screen chat the other day. I think she's come to terms with all of this being out in the open since the boys' appearance, so it seems to me. The things she went through - it's little wonder if she's still a bit insecure beneath it all.*

'*She seems to be unsure of herself and concerned about what they might be expecting, maybe. But that could well be just all that bloody baggage, from living with the stigma of being 'a Magdalene girl' - and those bloody nuns. Some of the poor women have never really recovered from that.*

'*Mammy had kept all that locked away for years and years - then it all came pouring out of her. It must have been such a release and she seems to be lighter in herself somehow recently, so she does. I just thank God those boys found each other - what's the odds of that ever happening? I'm so thankful that they did.*'

She drives into the short term car park, and locks Niall's car and walks into the terminal to greet them, self consciously holding on to her name boards.

Sinead checks the note on her phone with the flight numbers on the arrivals board, and it looks like the New York flight is early, so both flights are due in quite close together. She sends a message to both Gino and Jeannette to say where she's parked, just in case they miss each other. She positions herself by the exit in Arrivals, so they can see her when they come through.

Mam's Thoughts

"*What a day this is going to be. But what will these ladies think of me? I'm sure from what Sinead has said it will be grand. They both sound so nice.*

"*I can't wait to see those two lovely boys again as well - but how thoughtful of them to let us mothers have time to get to know each other first. It was great to have that call with the two of them on the laptop and I feel I know them a little bit now. I do so hope it all goes well.*

"*I'm only sad that I missed out on so many years of their lives but this is about catching up on all that - and celebrating that we're back in touch properly. I want to tell them how grateful I am for giving them both such a good life - they could have ended up anywhere - and what lovely young men they've turned them into.*

"I keep imagining what life would have been like if I'd gone back and stayed in Waterford. Despite the awfulness of the maternity home and that bloody Magdalene laundry, God-awful place so it was. Despite that, Dublin was an escape after all - into something of a life; I'm so thankful to Eileen to have the thought to put me up for those first few weeks until I'd gotten my own place. She became such a friend.

"Michael made my life complete - fancy him coming all that way just to find me again. And - not caring about me having been through all that. I am so blessed to have been loved like that - even now he's not so well. And how wonderful it was that he could meet and have some craic with the boys - all these years on.

"And dear Maireadh has been a trooper, helping me get this place bottomed and clean as a new pin for them coming. Oh my, oh my, I suppose all I can do is wait for them arriving..."

——————— ———————

Waiting in the Terminal 2 arrivals, Sinead watches all the waves and smiles of people coming through from baggage pickup, with expectation written on their faces, as they look out for their loved ones, friends, relatives. Some starting lives together, others coming to say goodbye to a family member perhaps. Each smile tells the story almost, it seems to her.

Jeannette's flight is the first one due and Sinead holds up a name card, just like the taxi drivers all around her. Jeannette spots her and waves - and they meet as she comes around the barriers - a little formally it feels as they shake hands - before making their way to the coffee shop to wait for the others arriving. The board shows their flight is due in 10 minutes, so plenty of time for coffee and a chat while they clear customs.

They see - and hear the two boys arriving with Angie, and they all hug before heading for the car park to pile all the luggage into the mini-van - and for Sinead to drive them to their hotel.

"Do you want to drop off your bags, and maybe settle in to freshen up? It's not far to Mam's, so we can be there in a jiffy."

"I'll not be long anyhow Sinead - I had a bit of sleep on the flight over and I just need to change."

"Same for me, Angie, I'll not be long. I just can't wait to meet your mother, Sinead."

Andy and Gino wave them off from the front steps of the hotel, as Sinead drives off.

Taking the short but momentous drive from the Beaumont, they pull up onto the front drive outside the neat cream painted house, Sinead smiling at Niall, standing in the open door to greet them, spots her Mam, Brenda, smiling broadly just behind his shoulder.

"Mammy, meet Angie and Jeannette."

End

Thanks

Huge thanks to Jim Nichols and Clare Tradgett for their ideas and input while editing the early drafts.

My thanks also to Shaun Best, and the members of the **'Write Here, Write Now'** group at the Storyhouse in Chester, for their observations and encouragement during my writing journey.

The Sean Mc Dermott Street Magdalene Laundry

(photo Julien Behal/PA Wire)

The Magdalene Laundries have been widely written about, since the practice was ended during the 1990s. Though this novel is about a fictitious character, Brenda's is a story that represents one that has played out many times over the decades of this institution's operation, for hundreds of women.

The **Open Heart City** website offers a comprehensive view of the institution:

> *"The twentieth-century Irish Magdalenes were punitive Institutions where socio-economically vulnerable girls and women were held under lock and key and forced into unpaid hard labour at laundry or needlework. The rationale for the incarceration was religious: girls of the Magdalene were frequently victims of rape and incest, and other girls and women were regarded as being guilty of or vulnerable to being sexually active outside the bonds of marriage. The Magdalene Institution was designed so that the girls and women confined there could do penance to*

*atone for the sexual sins that they were adjudged to have
committed or be in danger of committing."*

I have included the following selection of other resources which
readers may wish to explore.

Further Reading

Irish Times report on Magdalene restitution

Nuns who ran Magdalene laundries have not contributed to redress for women

Some €32m in awards of €11,000-€100,000 made to more than 800 survivors to date

Read more:
https://bit.ly/48Y3m0r

Opinion on the government response

Not Merely a Shameful Past: The Case for State Responsibility in the Magdalene Laundries

Victims of Magdalene Laundries have been denied their human right to redress

Read More:
https://bit.ly/3L77r8H

Open Heart City

History of Magdalene Institutions in 20th Century Ireland
Read More:
https://openheartcitydublin.ie/seanmcdermottstreet/

Justice for Magdalenes Research

A resource for people affected by and interested in Ireland's Magdalene institutions:
https://jfmresearch.com/books/dublinmagdalenelaundry/

Magdalene Laundry survivor (80) awarded settlement for unpaid work

Mary Cavner worked at the Good Shepherd's Convent in Co Cork following her father's death:

https://bit.ly/4o8zNxy

Small Things Like These

This film, as referenced by Niall in this story, was released 8 November 2024, with Cillian Murphy and Emily Watson. The film was based on the best-selling novel of the same name by **Claire Keegan**.

Film trailer:

https://youtu.be/Nqwn5Y_Y4xs?si=8Y-vQmT4_TKVtY7R

About Christopher Tradgett

Having spent many years copywriting in the affiliate marketing industry, a chance encounter with a writers group led Christopher to turn to writing fiction. The first publication was a short story, entered into local competitions, which was judged as in the Top 20% of entrants into the Oxford Flash Fiction Prize 2025.

Short Stories
The Scent of Death
Truck Stop